Turning Down Pie

A Crestfield Inn Romance

Elsie Davis

Sweet Romance Publishing

Sweet Romance Publishing

Sweetromancepublishing.com

PO Box 778

Liberty, NC 27298

Many thanks to Pastor Jenkins, his wife, and their lovely friends. I enjoyed meeting everyone while on my writer's camping retreat and was truly blessed when you invited me to join you for a campfire dessert. Broomsticks are totally delicious!

Psalm 133:1
How good and pleasant it is when God's people live together in unity.

Chapter One

❤

THE COLD BEAUTY OF an early morning ski slope, unmarred by skiers, was one of the most breath-taking sights Sally had ever seen. White snow glistening in the sun. And the thrill of finding the fall line and traversing it as tightly as possible was unparalleled. Skiers from around the world competed in several disciplines, but her favorite had always been downhill racing.

Getting from top to bottom in the fastest time possible, sometimes exceeding eighty miles per hour, was the ultimate in exhilaration. The need for speed wasn't something she had been able to resist since the first time she raced in an event at the age of nine—and won.

But this morning...none of the usual excitement filled her. Instead, trepidation and fear settled in the pit of her stomach as she spotted the chairlift.

She had come to Vermont, picking a smaller family-friendly ski resort for her first venture back on the slopes. The ride to the Bolton Valley Ski Resort was only ten minutes, but with each minute, she had started to second guess the sanity of what she was about to do. After studying the map last night to pick a suitable trail for her first time, Sally had felt somewhat better. But now, all confidence fled.

Sally forced herself to move forward, one gliding step at a time as her skis slid across the packed snow. The pain in her left leg intensified, but she tried to ignore it. Rehabbing after an injury was never easy. And this time was no exception.

Her last crash had taken its toll when the ski tip caught at the first gate in a slalom run, and she had tumbled down the mountainside, eventually skidding to a stop. It was a mistake that was totally her fault, and a costly one at that.

All that out of a practice run as she prepared for the opening day races in Austria.

Two surgeries and three months of rehab,
and what did she have to show for it? Her
private physician believed it was too risky
for her to ski professionally again. Her personal trainer thought she would be out for
at least a year. Her sponsors had pulled out
of their contracts, not wanting to hang their
hat on a professional skier who might never
ski again.

And then there was Addison Castle—her
father and coach. If he had his way, Sally
would have already been back out racing.
The word *poppycock* was his favorite expression when anyone told him otherwise.

Sally paused to rub her left knee and calf,
trying to ease the ache that never seemed
to go away. Fortunately, no one was in line
as she approached the Mid Mountain chair
lift. Tucking her poles under her arms and
stepping forward as the lift slowed, Sally
moved into position. Using her other hand,
she grabbed the sidebar to steady herself.
Then, pulling upward to ease the effort that
her leg would typically support for such a

simple move, she managed to land in the middle of the seat.

Much to her surprise, she wasn't alone. The other skier's presence forced her to shift to the left.

"Thanks," the man said, getting settled into position as they lowered the bar and the lift continued up the mountainside.

"No problem. I just didn't see you come up." Etiquette always ruled the day when it came to skiing—especially for a professional skier. She'd never been one to let it go to her head, preferring to remember that once upon a time, she was just learning. Even if it was when she was eight.

"Sorry. I just got here and was anxious to catch a ride to the top. You headed for the Glades or Beech Seal?" he asked, his warm breath hitting the air and forming a misty cloud of condensation.

A choice of two blue trails. Try neither.

Sally looked up at the man, giving him her full attention. And then wished she hadn't as she fought back a laugh at his Rudolph ski beanie, complete with a red pom-pom and antlers. The man had a foolish sense of humor, and his gear was archaic, but neither of those things detracted from his handsome good looks.

Judging someone by their gear was always a mistake. Her own gear, of course, didn't say never-ever or newbie, but that's precisely what her abilities might be today. Not having skied since the accident, she didn't know what to expect. Not that she'd admit anything to the stranger with eyes as blue as the sky. "The Glade to get warmed up." *Liar.* The green bunny trail was more her speed this morning.

"Great, so am I. Name's Randy Granger. I'm from Cedar Grove but only home on leave from the Army. Maybe we could ski down together. I haven't skied in years, and this could be interesting if you're in for a good laugh."

A man who didn't mind being the object of laughter was a rare thing. "Thanks, but I prefer to ski alone." *And down Bear Run...the shortest way back to the base of the mountain.* If anyone recognized her, it would be humiliation at its finest hour. Sally needed to get her ski legs and her confidence back, and it needed to happen in stages to coax her out of the place she'd retreated in her head. A place where she tumbled, over and over, the pain never-ending.

"Suit yourself." Randy shrugged. "I reckon you left your Christmas spirit at home this morning. Got a name besides Miss-Prefer-To-Ski-Alone?" he teased, his eyes crinkling with mirth.

She didn't have any Christmas spirit to leave at home, but it would seem Mr. Bright and Chipper had more than enough for the two of them. "Sally Chastain," she said, rolling her eyes at his weak attempt at humor, knowing he couldn't see through her goggles. At least she had remembered to use her mother's maiden name, not wanting anyone to recognize her. Twisting to the right slightly, Sally tried to send a subtle hint she preferred to keep to herself.

"So what brings you to Cedar Grove?" he asked, not taking the hint.

"Skiing...and you?" It was her turn to grin, knowing her answer was perfect. Why else would she be on the ski lift?

"Cute. A woman with a sense of humor. I like it. And likewise...skiing. Well, that and to make some decisions about my future in the Army. I'm thinking about getting out."

"Hope you figure it out. Enjoy the slopes," Sally said by way of dismissal. They drew close to the top, and she mentally prepared her exit, gripping her poles tight.

The chair slowed, and Randy raised the safety bar. "Maybe I'll see you again sometime. Nice chatting," he said, grinning.

The man was undaunted by any of her attempts to put him in his place with a don't-bother warning. "Maybe. Maybe not," she said, mustering the sweetest tone she could find.

Sally pushed off the seat, landed on her skis, and started to execute a sharp right to move away from the lift. Except Randy turned right, his skis catching in hers and throwing her off balance. An agonizing pain ripped through her knee, and she started to fall, her poles flailing in the air. Landing in a heap, she rolled to the side to get out of the way of the chair lift, hoping no one was behind them.

The alarm sounded, and the chairlift stopped. More attention Sally didn't need.

"I'm so sorry. Are you okay?" Randy asked, reaching out to help her up. "I'm guessing that was a dumb move. It's been a while, and I wasn't thinking. I should have gone left, right?"

That much was obvious. Sally grimaced against the pain, rubbing her leg and ignoring his outstretched hand. But, of course, it hadn't helped that her injury kept her from recovering from the fall and catching her balance like she might have in normal circumstances.

The lift operator came over and stepped in close. "Is everything okay here? Are you hurt anywhere?" he asked, kneeling down in the snow beside her.

Only her pride. "I'm fine," she snapped, mostly because she just wanted to be left alone to deal with the situation on her own, hoping no one would recognize her.

"It's nothing to be embarrassed about. Beginners do this all the time," the lift operator spoke, unaware of how much his words irked.

Sally pulled her hat down further and adjusted her goggles, relieved her face was almost entirely covered. "It's his fault," she said, pointing at Randy, unwilling to take the blame.

"It's true." Randy nodded. "I should have gone left, not right. I won't forget again, I promise."

"I'm not worried about whose fault it was; we just need to make sure everyone is okay and then keep moving. I've got to restart the lift."

Randy reached for her poles.

"Just leave them and go ski, please. I'm fine and can take care of myself." She was being unduly hard on him, but she had to make this scene end.

"Well, okay then. Guess that's putting me in my place." Randy shrugged, turned, and skied away toward the Glades trail. Pausing, he glanced back at her. "See you at the bottom," he called out and waved.

Randy was only trying to be friendly, but Sally wasn't looking for a friend. She was looking to discover if the doctor was right and if she'd ever ski again. None of that added up to small talk with a stranger or a day of fun on the slopes.

Today was day one, trying to find those answers. Determination propelled her to the top in skiing, and it was the same determination she needed to tap into now. Sally rolled to one side, using her right leg to help her stand, satisfying the liftie she was okay.

"Take it easy out there," he said before returning to the operator's station.

Only three other skiers had gathered around by the time Sally moved off toward the bunny trail. She could feel the eyes of the others on her and knew what they were thinking. *A never-ever.* It was always the beginner's fault.

With two World Cup titles, five Olympic medals, and twenty-three top ten finishes ...the last thing Sally Castle could be called was a beginner.

But then right now...she wasn't Sally Castle.

Chapter Two

♥

SALLY HAD EVERY RIGHT to be upset with him, and Randy couldn't get her pained expression out of his head. He had been a total idiot forgetting the rule of how to exit safely off the lift. But it wasn't his fault she wouldn't accept his help or his apology. That was all on her.

The rest of the morning, he had kept an eye out for her, but in his four runs down the Glades and Beech Seal trails, Sally had never resurfaced. The concern she was hurt more than she let on bothered him. And by the time Randy arrived home, he was convinced he had ruined her day and she'd left the ski resort as a result.

Granted there were many trails Sally could have taken, especially if she was trying to avoid him. But still, all routes ended up at the base of the mountain, and Randy had watched for her bright blue and pink ski jacket to come barreling down the mountainside. Several times.

Her outfit looked expensive and like it was straight out of a fashion ski shop. Her Rossignol skis appeared new, unlike his fifteen-year-old set. At some point, Randy would need to get new skis, but first, it would be a good idea to find out if he still enjoyed skiing. Ten years in the military hadn't allowed for any slope time. At best, his current skill level could be described as amateurish.

Randy pulled into the driveway of his mother's house, where he stayed during his military leave. Living at home for the duration wasn't ideal, but it made less sense for him to own a place until he knew for sure he was leaving the Army. A decision he had yet to make.

Right now, his focus was on getting through the holidays and taking care of Misty. Before his best friend died, Randy had promised to find the dog a new home.

Ben had loved Misty, but the military life wasn't a good mix for hauling a dog overseas, not to mention his friend's fiancé was allergic to dogs. The end result was Ben's grandparents kept watch over the Alaskan Husky in his absence, but they couldn't handle a dog Misty's size and her need for lots of exercise and youthful exuberance.

When Randy arrived home, he had visited Ben's grandparents to pick up Misty and bring her home with him. And since then, he'd grown quite fond of the Husky. It's almost as if they bonded together, sensing how much they each missed Ben. But, whatever it was, Randy was slow to look for a new owner, putting off the inevitable.

And if by any chance he didn't re-up, the idea had occurred to him that he would keep Misty. Owning a pet would be a first for him. A sense of responsibility he hadn't had before because of his childhood spent as an Air Force brat and then with his own life in the military.

Stomping his boots outside the front door to knock off any snow, he pulled the door open and went inside. The scent of Christmas pine and vanilla filled the air. Misty came running into the foyer and greeted him warmly, brushing up excitedly next to his leg and licking at his hand. "Hey girl," he said, patting her side.

His mother joined them. "You're home. How did it go?" she asked, reaching out to take his coat.

"It went okay, I guess. And I'll hang up my own coat. You taught me that skill when I was six." Randy grinned as he hung the jacket in the coat closet.

"That I did. But why was your day just okay? Did you fall a lot?" she asked, her teasing smile softening her face. His mother was a beautiful woman, and time had been good to her.

"Actually, no. Which was surprising, to say the least. But there was this woman, and I, ummm, sort of knocked her down."

His mother frowned. "Sort of? Either you did, or you didn't, so which is it?"

"I did. Accidentally though. Needless to say, I didn't make a good impression on Sally." He took his boots off and put them on the rubber mat to avoid making water puddles on the floor from any lingering snow clumps.

"Of course, it was accidental. I didn't think otherwise. So what's the problem? Let me guess, you didn't apologize. I thought I brought you up better than that?" she said, shaking her head.

"You did. And I did. Apologize, that is. Sally rejected it and wouldn't let me even help her to her feet." *Maybe he should have insisted.*

"Sounds to me like you did your best to make it right. So let it go, and don't let it spoil the rest of your day."

Good advice at any other time, just not today.

Misty followed him into the living room, lying at his feet when he sat in the recliner, close to the fire. "Right. But, the thing is, I can't get her expression out of my head. I'm worried I hurt her more than she let on, and it's bothering me. I really need to find out if she's okay. I didn't see her the rest of the morning, so I'm wondering if she left." He took a deep breath and exhaled, his gaze fixed on the stockings hung on the fireplace. A tradition his mother never stopped after he left home.

"That's a different story entirely. Do you know if this woman was a local or someone visiting the area?"

"Visiting for sure. Sally was dressed to the nines for a ski slope outing like she'd just stepped off a magazine shoot." Randy chuckled.

"You can't judge a book by its cover." She shook her head and frowned. "There are probably some very nice young ladies in town who know how to dress smart for any occasion, I'll have you know."

"I don't recall since the girls I knew from town were teenagers. Besides, Sally had a regular ski tag—not a local discount ticket." He winked. It was good to be home, the sights, sounds, and laughter a far cry better than what the barracks had to offer a single soldier.

She clipped him on the shoulder. "You rat. You could have led with that."

"And miss riling you up? Not a chance."

His mother huffed, but it rang insincere, her ensuing smile a better read on the situation. "Just remember, Santa's coming. If you're not a good boy, you'll end up on the naughty list."

"I probably stay there all the time anyway. Wouldn't want Santa to get the wrong idea by me suddenly appearing on the good list." The good times he and Ben had together never hurt anyone, but they did like to play practical jokes on some of the younger guys. Especially the privates straight out of boot camp.

Misty whined as if sensing Randy was thinking of Ben.

"*Tsk. Tsk.* You know you could always come to church with me and get on the right side of God and Santa," his mother said, glancing at him, a hopeful expression on her face.

"There is that. I promise I'll go with you to the candlelight service on Christmas Eve." Of course, it wouldn't change the outcome of the naughty or nice list with Santa, but Randy was hoping he would find more peace regarding his friend's death and his own indecision about his future with the military.

"You need to apologize to the woman," his mother said, suddenly changing the subject back.

Based on history, Randy's alarm bells went off whenever his mother circled back to a finished conversation. "I told you, I already did," he countered.

His mother shot him one of her know-it-all smiles. "I mean, apologize *again*. You want to fix this, and you want to know how she's doing, and I've got the most delicious idea. Apology pie. You still know how to cook, don't you?" she teased.

Randy hadn't made a pie in over ten years. "I don't know. It's been a long time." And more than likely, if he did make one and deliver it, she'd more than likely deliver it right back to him...*in his face.*

"If she's not from around here, chances are she's staying in town or over in Willow Springs. Between the two, there's a limited number of places you could call to see if you can pinpoint her location. Then, you could make her your world-famous strawberry-rhubarb pies." His mother was all in with the idea, her voice animated.

An animation Randy couldn't match. "World famous is a stretch."

"Cedar Grove famous then. You did win a 4-H cooking competition with it," she insisted.

Randy groaned. "Don't remind me." He had been teased for years after that and eventually dropped out of the 4-H. Something he regretted, but at the time, it felt right. "But I will take your idea and give it a whirl."

"Good for you, son. And when you head over to the Crestfield Inn, you can start by checking there for Sally."

Calling around made more sense and would be a lot less time-consuming. "Don't you mean I can start by calling the Crestfield Inn to see if she's there?"

"No." She crossed the room to stand in front of the Christmas tree, a pensive look on her face. "I hope you don't get upset at me, but I need you to stay there for a while. At the Crestfield Inn, that is."

"You're kicking me out of the house?" he asked, stunned by the request.

She shook her head. "Nonsense. It's not kicking you out when I ask nicely, and it's only temporary. Your sister is having problems with her pregnancy, and they are taking her out of work. She's going to come to stay here because her husband is gone so much with his job. He'll come here of course when he's in town." His mother readjusted a few decorations on the tree as if uncomfortable with the big ask she had just laid at his feet.

"Why can't she use her old room? It's bigger." It wasn't high on his priority list to go anywhere else as he was enjoying being in his own home.

"I need your room for Naomi and Matt because your aunt and uncle are due in tomorrow, and they need the other room until after Christmas. There's no sense getting your sister settled in one room and then having to move her. You know how your aunt is particular about having a private bath when she visits. So I called the inn, and they had a cancellation. I went ahead and booked it for you. And Mr. Montpelier, the owner, said it was fine for you to bring Misty."

It sounded like his mother had all the details worked out, and the only thing she needed was his approval. But then she knew he wouldn't say no. "This doesn't sound like a few days."

"Until after the Christmas holidays. I think your aunt and uncle are leaving the day after Christmas. Please tell me you're okay with this. I hate to ask, but I don't see as there's much choice."

"I'll expect extra presents and a giant-sized portion of Christmas ham." The more he thought about it, the less he minded. A houseful of people underfoot didn't do much for him, while the peace and quiet of the inn held far greater appeal. Military life had prepared him to be ready for quick changes. Apparently, even on leave, those qualities would serve him well.

His mother hugged him, dropping a kiss on his cheek. "Thank you for being so understanding. You always were a good kid."

"Yeah, yeah. I had a good teacher. But don't forget the extra gifts." Randy chuckled. He wasn't really looking for more presents, but it had become a joke ever since the time his mother had tried to bribe him to watch his sister until she got home from work.

Giving up the boy scouts hadn't been a hardship, not that Randy had told his mother. But he also hadn't been willing to accept the money she offered for babysitting. After the fact, he decided it was more a case of stupidity because what young boy didn't need money? But Randy liked to think it was based on good character—a trait that had stood him in good stead all his life.

After going to the store for what he needed for the strawberry-rhubarb pie, Randy spent the next hour and a half baking in the kitchen. It wasn't his best effort, but it certainly wasn't his worst. There were a few tricks he'd remembered too late, but overall, he was pleased with the result. Of course, the upside to all his efforts was that if he couldn't find Sally, he would have the pie all to himself.

"Ready to go?" he asked Misty, who lay curled up by the door.

Woof. Woof. The dog got up, excited for an adventure outdoors. Either that or a chance at the pie. Something else his friend had mentioned—the dog had a sweet tooth and was known for sneaking a dessert or two, or three.

Thinking of Ben always had the power to sadden him. His buddy had been ready for life and love and to settle down with his fiancé, but then tragedy struck. Now, it would never happen. The reality had hit Randy hard, and it was the reason he was considering leaving the military. It might be too late for Ben, but it wasn't too late for Randy. The idea of finding love and having a family wasn't something he had considered before, but Ben had opened his eyes to the possibility. His friend's joy and happiness had been an almost tangible aura, and something Randy hadn't been able to deny. To the point he had become envious, wanting some of the same joys in life.

Randy loaded up the car and headed for the Crestfield Inn. The old 1700s home was one of the largest in the area and one used as an inn for travelers and locals alike since back in the 1800s. If the walls could talk, he was certain there would be lots of stories to tell. The newest owner had turned the place into a bed and breakfast a few years ago while Randy was away.

It wasn't far from the house, and soon he was turning into the long freshly plowed driveway. He parked where several other vehicles had lined up and then made his way to the front porch. Misty was having a good time playing in the snow beside him. Her playful barks as she chased a squirrel made Randy laugh at the antics. In the deep snow, the dog didn't stand a chance of catching up to the little critter.

The outside of the three-story house was decorated with Christmas wreaths, white lights, and even a nativity scene, adding to the ethereal beauty of the place. Christmas always added a little magical wonder.

With only one duffel bag for his belongings, it was a simple matter to juggle it and the pie. He pulled open the door and entered, the scent of cinnamon and apples hitting him straight away, reminding him of home. A large tree stood in the corner, decorated with bright, colorful balls and bows and topped with an angel. Poinsettias graced every table.

Randy glanced around and approached the front desk. He rang the little bell on the counter.

"Hello, hello. So sorry I was in the back when I heard you arrive. My name's Kyle." The young man glanced down at the dog, a broad grin on his face. "And I reckon you must be Randy Granger, and this cutie is Misty." Kyle came around the counter and kneeled to pet the dog.

Misty, of course, was more than happy to lap up the attention.

"Yes, I'm Randy." He set the pie on the counter to sign the register.

"Perfect. Let me get you logged into the computer and get your keys. I've got you on the second floor. I had only gotten the cancellation an hour before your mother called. Talk about luck. Anyway, we have quiet hours after nine for the other guest's comfort. I'm not sure if you'll be needing dining services or going home to eat. But if you want to eat here, we have the Garden Delight Bistro, just down the hall toward the back of the house. It overlooks the gardens, of course." Kyle pointed in the direction of the café. "Not that you can see any flowers this time of year, but there are lots of beautiful evergreens," he added.

"Breakfast is included in your stay, and the restaurant is open Thursday to Sunday for dinner. I recommend reservations, especially this time of year with the skiers and snow-bound vacationers that flock to the area. Otherwise, there's Bixby's diner, Murphy's, or Cade's Tavern." Kyle stopped suddenly and frowned. "I'm sorry. I'm betting you know all that as well. It's a habit that's hard to break as most all my guests need to hear about these places."

Randy slid the clipboard back across the desk. "It's all good. I'm only recently back in town, so a refresher course doesn't hurt."

"Here's your key. Room seven. Up the stairs and to the right. Is that your mother's parting gift since she booted you from your own room?" Kyle teased, eyeballing the pie with interest.

He shook his head. "Actually, no. This is an Apology pie, and I'm hoping you can tell me if someone is staying here at the inn." Of course, anywhere other than a small town, confidentiality laws might make his search for Sally more difficult. But in a town the size of Cedar Grove...people liked to talk.

"Who are you looking for?" Kyle asked.

"Sally Chastain. Woman about five-seven, blonde hair. I'm trying to give her this pie if I can find her," Randy said, hoping to reassure Kyle his intentions were good.

"What did you do?" Kyle grinned. "Stand her up on a date, did you?"

"No. Actually, I knocked her flat on her keister."

"I see. And you forgot to apologize." Kyle stated the obvious, but it didn't happen that way at all.

"No. I did that too, but she wasn't interested. I just need to make sure she's okay, and my mother thought this would be a good way to find out."

"Your mother's a smart woman. And you're in luck as Sally Chastain is staying here."

Bingo. And on the first try. "Can you tell me what room?" Randy asked, excited at the prospect of seeing her again and making sure there were no adverse effects from the fall.

"*Hmmm.*" Kyle's face scrunched up as he considered the request. "I'm not sure that's a good idea. Privacy and all."

"Please?" Randy urged, picking up the pie.

"Well, okay. Seeing as you're a local and come bearing gifts. Most bad guys wouldn't bring pie." Kyle grinned, relaxing once again.

"Especially not a pie they personally baked," Randy added for good measure.

Kyle's mouth dropped open in a wide "O". "Really? She's in room four. The same floor as you, so I reckon you would have run into her anyway. And you're in luck, as I know she's currently in residence."

"Thanks, Kyle."

Randy headed up the stairs, Misty following close behind. The door to his room stood open, and he went inside. Impressed was a mild word for what he felt. It was like stepping back in time. Antiques decorated the room, and the old hand-carved poster bed looked inviting. The dresser and end table were also handmade. Heavy brocade curtains lined the windows. He set his duffel bag down. "Sit tight, Misty, and I'll be right back." The sooner he took care of this, the sooner he could relax for the evening.

Woof. Woof.

He picked up the pie and headed for Sally's room, trying to find the right words. *Hey, it's me again*, didn't seem to say the right thing. *Hey, I hope you like pie because I thought you could use some sweetening.* That comment would earn him a pie in the face for sure...something he would deserve if he made such a rude comment. But then, no matter what he said, he might end up with a pie in the face.

Chapter Three

♥

K*NOCK. K*NOCK.*

The sound startled Sally as she wasn't expecting visitors. No one knew where she was—not even her father. She debated answering the door but decided it was overkill on precautionary measures. For all she knew, it could be Kyle from the front desk delivering tomorrow's daily itinerary or some such nonsense. Of course, they were nothing she would be taking part in, but still, the man would simply be doing his job.

Without a peephole, opening the door was her only choice. Sally was shocked to discover it wasn't Kyle, but in fact, Randy. The skiing disaster without his skis. "Oh, good grief." She couldn't imagine why he was here. Or could she? There was nothing that needed to be said between them unless it explained why he was following her. The thought made her nervous and she started to shut the door.

"Wait," Randy said, putting a hand on the door to stop her.

"Why?" she asked, managing to deliver a frigid ring in her voice so that he would make no mistake she wasn't impressed by his appearance. If he was following her, then it made sense he knew who she was. Maybe Randy wasn't in the military at all, and he was just another reporter trying to get the inside scoop.

"This is for you." Randy held out a pie, the aroma of strawberry wafting toward her. "My mother calls it Apology pie. Otherwise known in this case as Strawberry-Rhubarb pie. I'm trying to apologize again for knocking you down this morning. I felt awful, and clearly, you hadn't forgiven me. I was worried you were hurt worse than you were letting on. So I decided to make an effort to reassure myself you were okay," Randy said, rambling on and not giving her a chance to end the conversation.

"I'm fine. I don't need your apology, and please leave me alone. How did you find me anyway? Are you following me? I'll call the police if I see you here again." *That should put him in his place.*

Randy drew back as if stung, a deep frown etched on his face. "*Ummm*, why would you call the police? I'm not sure delivering a pie is against the law. But then again, crazier laws have managed to survive time all over the county. And as to not seeing me again, that's going to be kind of hard considering I'm staying here at the Crestfield Inn."

He was staying here. Something wasn't adding up. "You told me you were a local. Now suddenly you're a guest at the same bed & breakfast I'm staying at. What's up with that?" Her heart hammered loudly as she tried to piece together what he said and his true motive for showing up at her door.

Randy nodded. "Both are true. I am a local. I told you I'm home on leave, and actually, I was staying at my mother's. But with the holidays just around the corner and family due to arrive, my mother wanted me to stay here at the inn as we're tight on space. It would seem my pregnant sister, who's having complications I might add, managed to usurp my room."

Which all sounded plausible until he tossed in the pregnant sister with complications. The more complicated the story, the more likely a lie. Something she had learned early on when trying to read people and deciding who was a friend and who was a foe. Or to figure out who simply wanted to use her fame to catapult their own rise to the top. Something that happened far more often than Sally had ever gotten used to. "I see. In that case, have a nice evening. Thanks for stopping by. Oh, and take your pie with you." Sally didn't need gifts that came with strings attached.

Except Randy hadn't mentioned any strings. Not yet anyway. "Just what is it you're after?" she asked, hoping to make him slip up and reveal why he was really here.

"Nothing more than your forgiveness. Like I said, I wanted to make sure you were okay." His eyes spoke of genuine sincerity, leaving Sally to wonder if she was overreacting.

It was a silly accident and one that wouldn't have been anything more than a mild embarrassment if it weren't for her bum leg and the pain the fall had caused. Which had nothing to do with Randy. "Fine, you're forgiven. As you can see, no lasting issues from this morning's fall. Now you can leave me alone."

He nodded. "Well, okay then." Randy stepped back. "Oh, and one other thing. I'm sorry in advance if my dog barks, but it's a new place, and Misty is a bit excitable. Hopefully, she'll settle down after I take her out for a walk."

A dog. This just kept getting better. "I'll survive," she said. Sally loved dogs. In fact, she'd always wanted one, but with training and racing, it was never the right time. She wondered what kind of dog the macho-military guy would have—most likely a macho German Shepard.

Randy held out the pie. "You should have this. I made it for you."

"Made or bought?" Not that it mattered...pie wasn't on her list of approved foods for a healthy diet. Hadn't been in years.

"Made fresh and still slightly warm," he countered, surprising her.

The more she learned about Randy, the more he intrigued her. And there was no room for intrigue in her life. "Thank you, but I can't," she said, wishing her answer could be different. The pie's fruity fragrance had teased her sense the whole time they stood at the door and her stomach was on high alert.

"Suit yourself. But I'll just set it here on the table in case you change your mind." Randy laid it down, turned, and walked away. *All of two doors down*. He waved before he disappeared into the room, an excited bark greeting him.

At least that much of his story was true.

Sally closed the door. It was almost dinner, and she needed protein-heavy foods, not sweet desserts—no matter how tempting. *Comfort pie*. That's what her mother used to call them when she baked pies fresh for

Sally after a rough day at school. Something she hadn't thought of in years. Not since she was eight. Not since her mom died.

Desperate times called for desperate measures.

Pulling the door open, she peeked out. The coast was clear, and Sally snatched up the pie and retreated inside the room. Covered in plastic wrap and adorned with red and white Christmas ribbon that held the plastic fork, knife, and napkin in place. Randy had thought of everything.

Just one piece, she promised herself, digging in to cut a slice. Without a plate, she ate straight from the pie tin. Call it a guilty pleasure, but her father wasn't here to see her and admonish her choices. "*Hmmm*," she groaned, savoring bite after bite. The sweet and tart flavors blended together perfectly, whetting her appetite for more.

It was hard to believe Randy baked this. His mother perhaps, if that part of his story was factual, but not him.

Her phone rang, the ring tone alerting her it was Jessica. Her best friend on and off the circuit, the two shared everything. Just not the pie because she wasn't here. Sally grinned, taking another bite before answering. "Hey there. What's up?" Her friend supported her decision to retreat to a private location. And it was Jessica who threw the media off her scent so Sally could disappear off their radar.

"Everything. But first, tell me about you. How's it going so far? Have you tried to ski yet?" Jessica asked.

"I haven't been here but two days. And I did try this morning, but it didn't work. But that's because another skier ran into me on the lift. My leg gave out, and I was done for by the time I reached the bottom of the hill. So I came back to my room to ice the leg. I'll try again tomorrow after I've rested it a bit."

"That stinks. Your dad keeps bugging me for your whereabouts. He's not a happy dude."

Using her mother's maiden name made it easy to slip into her new role and hide from the world. From Sally Castle, world-famous professional skier, to Sally Chastain, a nobody who couldn't handle a bunny slope without falling. Although, that was partly Randy's fault. *And her bum leg.*

"I'm sure. But I can't take the pressure to perform anymore. I need to figure this out on my own. My future that is. Another endorsement dropped off. The longer I'm off the circuit, the more expensive this will get for my dad. We've been through all that early on, and I'm not certain it's worth it this late in the game. We all know I've only got a few years left at best. These young women coming up in the ranks are filled with determination, and they have youth and flexibility on their side." It was the same issue every skier faced. *When to call it quits.* And for Sally, it was time. Or almost. The idea of quitting after a crash didn't sit well with her. That's why she had to try this. *On her own and at her own pace.* Ultimately, only she knew what she was capable of doing—the rest were just guessing.

"True story. Megan Foster is one to keep an eye on for sure. Take your time to decide. There's no rush, and you know it," Jessica said.

"My father doesn't agree." Her friend was the person who understood her the best and understood the fears and the challenges she would face to make a comeback. *If she made one.*

"But this is your future, not your father's. So what have you done since you didn't ski? Experience life a bit while you can. Unfortunately, our grueling schedule doesn't allow for much of that, and yet, we both know it's important," Jessica added.

There was no excuse for not getting out and exploring the town other than the most obvious one. "I sat in my room. Not much fun there, I know. But I'm afraid of being seen."

"*Arghhh.* Cover up, girl. Get out of the room and do something for fun. That's an order."

Sally took another bite of pie. "How about this for fun... I'm eating a freshly baked pie." It was almost mean to tell her friend, knowing neither of them ever enjoyed such treats.

"You don't eat pie. What brought this on?"

"I do now, and because I can. Oh, and because it was delivered personally by this handsome man. And who, by the way, also happens to be the same guy who knocked me over on the slopes this morning." Sally grinned, giving Jessica a few seconds for the comment to sink in.

"Whoa, wait a minute. You need to start from the beginning."

Sally obliged, and by the time she was finished relaying the story, she'd consumed the second piece of pie. "So much for dinner. Two pieces down, two to go. Best dinner ever." She'd pay for this tomorrow, but for tonight...why not?

"That's only four. What happened to the other half of the pie?"

"They were really big pieces." Sally laughed. *Big, comfort pieces.* Her mother was right, and it was working wonders on her lagging spirit. "So what's going on in the ski world behind the scenes?"

"Oh, you know. The same old stuff. Training. Practice runs. Calisthenics. And Repeat. Everyone is gearing up for the Olympics in February," Jessica said. "Ten to twelve hours a day and no rest for the weary, especially with the World Pro Ski Tour in full swing now."

Sally's stomach twisted in knots at the mention of the WPST. She'd waited a long time for a pro women's race to be scheduled in Vail, her hometown course. And now it looked like she wouldn't even be able to ski in it. It was less than three weeks away. There simply wasn't enough time to rehab correctly and get past her fears. It was all so disheartening. "Don't remind me. I love the slopes at Beaver Creek, and the fall line loves me."

"And don't I know it. You beat me out by seven-tenths of a second, you ski bum." Jessica laughed.

The comment would have been made with sheer envy or jealousy from anyone else but not her friend. Instead, they supported each other every step of the way. In fact, if it hadn't been for Jessica, Sally might have quit skiing years ago, the joys and thrill of the challenge waning.

"It's not like you haven't done the same to me," Sally teased, knowing that every skier had good days and bad days. Some simply had more good than bad, like Lindsey Vonn. That woman could ski like nobody's business. She would forever go down in the history books as one of the greatest skiers of all time.

"So, what's going on with Bobby?" Sally asked, wondering why Jessica hadn't mentioned him yet. Usually, her friend was full of Sally's so-called boyfriend's exploits. Jessica didn't like him much, although she didn't interfere. It's not like there was time for anything serious...but it was nice to have someone to go on a date with every now and then.

"He's a bum. I keep telling you to just forget him," Jessica said, her voice taking on an edge.

There was way more to the story. "Why? You can't just say that and not tell me more. What did he do now?" Sally asked, knowing that with Bobby there would always be more to a story. The man liked to live in the spotlight.

Jessica left out a deep sigh. "He's seeing someone else."

"Well, okay then. That should make you happy. We were good friends who went out on a few dates. I thought things were headed in a more serious direction after he kissed me once, but then the accident happened. So it's not like I expected him to stick around." Although, that didn't mean his defection didn't hurt.

"I'm sorry. I know you liked the jerk."

"But you didn't, so it's all good. Apparently, you're a better judge of character than I am. It's the nature of what we do on the circuit. The publicity aspects. The pressures. Things change, and the uncertainty of everything in my life is definitely a reason for him to change course." Sally was trying to justify it to herself, even if it didn't sound that way.

"That's not love; it's lust," Jessica quipped. "You deserve so much better."

"You're right."

"Listen, I've got to run. But keep me posted how tomorrow goes, and if you run into Mr. Handsome Clumsy, be sure to say hi for me. Maybe you can put in a good word, and he'll make me a pie if I come to visit." Jessica laughed.

"Will do." Sally hung up the phone and moved to the window. Down below, she noticed a man and a dog returning to the inn. Randy. And the dog was no German Shepard. Instead, it was a beautiful Siberian Husky, and the two of them played like best friends. It looked more like he was on the up and up, and she'd been harsh in her judgment.

Unfortunately, there was nothing she could do about it now.

Well, except to enjoy the rest of his pie.

Chloe turned to Captain Tremont. "What do you make of all that nonsense?"

Captain Tremont let out a husky laugh. "Probably not what you make of it, and I'm smart enough to wait for you to tell me. You haven't been wrong yet."

"You flatter me, my dearest Captain, and yes, I do have an opinion. I think that woman Sally has

something troubling going on, and she's looking for answers. I also think she wants to like Randy but doesn't trust him. Or anyone else, for that matter. On the other hand, Randy openly likes the girl, or why would he bake her a pie? Apology pie was an excuse to see her again, and we both know it." Chloe moved to the center of the room, closer to the captain.

"That part I totally agree with. I would have never made a pie to get your attention." He winked, bowing low before her. "Flowers or per-haps a delicate fan are more suited to your love-liness, my dear."

"This is the twenty-first century, my dearest Captain. You must think outside the 1800's box. I'm not even sure women use fans anymore. Such a shame as they were good for flirting," she teased.

"Yes, I seem to remember you using the tech-nique quite effectively with me." The captain winked.

"And then my twin sister did the same, and you were smitten with her," Chloe said, playfully tapping his shoulder.

"My greatest folly, and one for which I am eternally grateful you managed to fix. That and

making sure my military honor was restored. For without that, I would have never been good enough for my one true love—you." He kissed the back of her hand.

"Flattery will get you everywhere. But right now, it would seem we have a new romance brewing. Or there would be one if the two of them got out of each other's way long enough to get to know one another. We need to pay attention and make sure they do."

"If you say true love is on the horizon, I believe you. You were right about us and right about the others. As a matchmaker, you're one of the best."

"One of the best?" Chloe laughed. "I'm the only one you know. And you, my dearest Captain, are my assistant."

Captain Tremont took her by the arm, and they floated up the stairs to the attic. It was time for their nightly waltz.

Chapter Four

♥

RANDY ATE BREAKFAST AT the Garden Delight Bistro, the chef's special none other than one of his favorites. Eggs benedict wasn't something he often got while serving in the military. Being on leave, however, was another story. He lingered over his meal, enjoying every last morsel, but truth be told, he was watching for Sally.

With no sign of Sally on the slopes or at the inn since their last encounter, he finally gave up looking. The woman was as prickly as a pear, but it hadn't stopped him from thinking about her. Not that she wanted to be friends, her opinion on the matter was quite clear. Next time, perhaps he should make her a pear cake.

Next time? He chuckled. He doubted there would be a next time to cook her anything. Although, he was more than a little curious about what happened to the pie. It had disappeared by the time he had come back out of the room to take Misty for a long walk, which had only been minutes later.

The morning air was brisk, and he pulled his jacket a little tighter around the collar. Driving to the resort, he made his plan of attack for today's agenda. As much as he wanted to take it up a notch, he wasn't so sure he was ready after all the years he had been gone. Somehow, the snow felt icier, the ground harder when he managed to fall, and the cold seeped through to his bones that much faster. But the worst, was the aching muscles by the time he got home after a full day. He'd stick with the blue trails of Beech Seal and the Glades, choices that had nothing to do with Sally Chastain. *Or maybe a little.*

There weren't many people in line for the lift yet, and it wasn't long before he was standing at the top of the slope, surveying the scene below.

A few skiers were making the best of another clear, sunshiny day to heat the air and make for top-notch ski weather.

Randy pushed off and headed down the slope, cutting back and forth with the edge of his skis and using the pizza wedge to slow himself down when needed. He rather valued staying upright as he sped down the mountainside. Or *eased* down the mountainside as the case might be. The cold was exhilarating. The feeling of being in control of his destiny was satisfying, even if fleeting.

You weren't in control of what happened in the military unless you were an officer or other high-ranking enlisted soldier. Joining straight out of high school, college hadn't been in his plans until much later. And by the time he'd completed his degree online, he wasn't much interested in power and authority, just doing his job. As a combat soldier, it was vital to remain focused if one wanted to stay alive and out of trouble. But it was also where Randy felt he was doing the best for his country and his platoon.

He turned to the lifts at the bottom of the hill, ready to catch another ride up. Randy spotted a woman with a blue and pink jacket headed in the same direction. He picked up his pace, unable to resist another chance to talk with Sally and ask about the pie.

"Good morning," he said, pulling up next to her.

"You again?" Sally asked, shooting him a frown. "Now I'm really wondering if I should be worried."

Randy chuckled. "You don't. It's purely co-incidence, trust me. Not the other day, with the pie and all. There aren't many places you could stay around here and you being at the Crestfield Inn was dumb luck when Kyle confirmed you were staying there." It was important to him that she believed it was all true, although why he cared so much wasn't anything he wanted to put under a microscope.

"Fate, huh? In that case, good morning." She eyed him carefully, her words say-ing one thing, but clearly, she wasn't quite ready to jump on the trust train with him yet.

"So, *ummm*, I noticed the pie was gone when I took Misty for a walk. Did you enjoy it?" he asked, going with the assumptive close and catching her off guard.

Sally grinned. "I see I'm busted. I did enjoy it, so thank you. You didn't have to make it. If you really did, that is. My bet's on your mom."

"Stay away from Vegas and the lottery." Randy chuckled. "Your bet would be wrong. Two cups sliced strawberries, two cups chopped rhubarb, two cups sugar...but I only use a quarter cup. Too sweet is never good. And let's see, there's a teaspoon of—"

"Okay, stop. I believe you," Sally said, shaking her head as they neared the lift.

"Do you trust me to do this again? Ride the lift together, I mean? I promise not to turn the wrong way." Randy was pushing his luck, but on such a beautiful day, why not? The worst she could say was no.

"It's not like I have much choice. Either that or the liftie will shoot us an evil eye for taking up two lifts," Sally said, stepping forward as the lift slowed, leaving him to follow—or not.

He'd take it as a yes. Randy moved carefully into place and held the safety bar up as Sally jumped on the chairlift. They settled into place, and he lowered the bar as the lift picked back up in speed, on its way to the top.

"Are you doing Beech Seal?" he asked, hoping to convince her to ski with him. Skiing with a friend was always more fun, or it used to be.

Sally hesitated. "I guess," she said, shrugging as if it didn't matter.

Maybe she was interested in skiing together and had truly forgiven him. It was a nice thought. "After you're warmed up, we could take the Vista Quad up if you want to ski the Vista Glade trail. I haven't been on a black trail in a long time, but I'm game if you are. I'm working on getting my ski legs back but skiing with you sounds like fun." He would more than likely make a fool of himself, but it was worth the risk to spend some time with Sally.

"No, no. Beech Seal is fine. But I don't remember agreeing to ski with you. I like to ski alone. Sorry."

Talk about a letdown. It was like riding a rollercoaster since he had first knocked Sally off her feet. "I just thought since you enjoyed my pie, it was a fair trade."

"The pie was an apology, not a friendship offering." Sally shot him a smile, and as soon as they arrived at the top, she hopped off the chair and headed for the trail. "See you at the bottom," she said, sliding her goggles into place and pushing off.

Randy followed suit, undaunted by the brush-off. He sailed past her, the thrill of the ride taking over as he headed down the mountain, this time a little faster than the last. When he reached the bottom, he turned to watch for Sally's approach, but didn't see her. But then, the skiers were like tiny ants careening down the slope at this point, the resort getting busier.

Shoving aside his disappointment, he made his way to the lift. One last run, and he might just be ready to test his hand, or his legs in this case, on Vista Glades. It was the easiest black diamond trail on the slope but the most challenging trail he'd done as a youngster.

He started down the mountain. Catching a glimpse of Sally off to the side of the trail and close to the out-of-bounds area, he noticed she wasn't moving. Randy cut his edges to turn hard and fast, traversing to the right, and coming to a quick stop, the snow spraying into the air. "Are you okay?" he asked, moving close.

"Just dandy. Thanks anyway," Sally said, giving him another brush-off.

At some point, he should give up on her, but he wasn't quite at that point yet. There was something about her that kept making him want to know more and to get through the gruff exterior. "Well, come on then. You can't seem to get rid of me, so you might as well join me."

"Fine," Sally ground out, giving in ungraciously. "I've got to get down this hill at some point unless I want the ski patrol to cart me off." Pain and anger, and frustration laced her voice.

"We'll take it slow." Randy waited for her to start out and then followed, letting her set the pace. Then, finally, it occurred to him that just because she had designer equipment and apparel did not mean she could ski.

Sally had all the right moves, so she had some experience. And he was no expert, but perhaps he could offer her some advice. As long as she was more receptive to his help than she was to his pie. *But then, she did end up liking it.* The thought gave him the courage to speak up.

They finished the trail and came to a stop at the bottom. Randy took off his goggles and moved closer to Sally. "That was fun," he said, easing into the conversation.

"From whose perspective? Certainly not mine," she ground out, breathing harder than one would expect. She glanced around the area as if searching for something...or someone.

"I'm no expert, but if you'd like, I might be able to give you a few pointers. I mean, you were doing really good, just some mechanics seemed off," Randy explained, not wanting to offend her.

Sally shook her head and laughed. "Lessons? I think I'll pass." The derision was back in her voice, but it was teamed up with something that mildly resembled humor.

"Everyone needs to learn sometime if they want to get better. Don't look at it like it's an insult. Just one friend helping another."

"Okay, then...humor me. What should I do?" It was the tone of her voice that irritated him, as it was borderline condescending.

And he wasn't the one who just came down the mountain at a snail's pace. "For starters, stay down lower. It keeps the center of your gravity moving faster and yet more on the stable side. Also, don't be afraid to speed up, and then use the pizza wedge to slow you down to a comfortable point when you feel you're going too fast." He would start with the basics and build, not wanting to overwhelm her at this point.

"Anything else, Mr. Ski Instructor?"

Randy took off his ski cap and ran a hand through his hair. "Try having fun," he said, shooting her a grin. His reluctant new friend needed to lighten up.

"Fun. Now there's a new tip I've never heard before. Or at least not in forever." Sally headed toward the lodge, ignoring his suggestion and giving up for the day. She pulled the collar of her coat up around her neck and her hat down low but didn't bother to remove the goggles that would have impeded the walk back to the lodge.

Which was odd since she wasn't making another run. It was almost as if she didn't want to be seen. *Or recognized.* Randy followed. "Want to get a cup of coffee?" he asked.

"No. That's it for me today."

Message received. Leave me alone.

Except now that he was positive he was on the right track to figuring her out...he was determined to do just the opposite. Maybe she had a jealous ex-boyfriend she was hiding from. He hadn't noticed a wedding ring—not that it ruled out a husband. Add to that her worry he was following her meant there was a good chance she was in trouble.

Sally's message was loud and clear, but it didn't mean Randy intended to follow her rules. If anything, it meant he would keep a closer eye on her—his protective streak in high alert.

Chapter Five

♥

A QUICK GLANCE IN the mirror left Sally feeling as though she looked too much like Sally Castle and not enough like someone else entirely. Pulling her hair into a bun, she stuck a clip in it, going for a more refined look. She donned a fake pair of eyeglasses, hoping to add to the secretarial image. Without her ski goggles, it would be far too easy for someone to recognize her. Satisfied, she headed downstairs to the bistro.

After she had returned to the inn yesterday, the day was a bust. Left alone, she went over and over what could possibly be wrong with her technique. Her aching leg was a part of the problem, but it was almost as if she was a different person on the slopes altogether. When she'd come to Cedar Grove under an alias, she hadn't expected to leave behind her skiing talents as well.

Somewhere in the middle of the night, the answer hit her and it wasn't good. In fact, it was one of the worst things that could happen to a professional skier. *Fear.* Her lack of confidence was grounded in fear and it was controlling her every move. The inability to let loose and trust her finely-honed instincts was non-existent. The result...failure.

And there was only one way to fix the problem, and that was to keep skiing. She would have to force herself to take risks on the slopes, challenging herself until instinct took over.

Tackling the blue run right away had been foolish, but there was no way she could do the bunny trail knowing Randy was right there. Pride may had gotten in her way, but thankfully, it turned out okay. Not to mention, his offer to give her pointers was the proof she needed to finally trust that Randy was on the up and up and was clueless about her identity. He had no ulterior motive in seeking her out other than friendship.

Something she could use right about now. And if she skied with Randy and let him teach her, it would be the perfect cover. She would simply be a novice learning how to ski, and no one would be any wiser if she kept a low profile.

At one point, she'd even considered dying her hair, but that seemed a bit over the top. Now she wouldn't need to. There was no sign of Randy or Misty as she headed for the bistro. "Good morning, Kyle," she said, spotting him by the Christmas tree.

"Good morning, Sally. I see you're headed for breakfast this morning. Good choice. Chef James has a special—poached eggs with avocado and Boursin cheese on an English muffin. One of my favorites." He grinned, moving to the table to straighten some flyers.

"Sounds good. I like the sound of all three. Can't say as I've eaten them together like that, though. Oh, by the way...has *ummm*, Randy Granger come through here this morning?"

Kyle stopped what he was doing to look up at her. "Yes, why do you ask?"

Sally blushed. It wasn't a question she had a ready answer for. "As you know, he brought me a pie. I wanted to thank him." Of course, she had already done that, but it was as good an excuse as any. Admitting she needed Randy for any other reason would require an explanation, one that would give away far more information than she planned to give. To anyone. *Including Randy.*

"He's already in the dining area. Arrived perhaps five minutes ago, so you're in luck." Kyle grinned, the man reading far too much into the situation.

"Great. Thanks." Sally moved off down the hall, her heart racing as she glanced around the bistro in search of Randy.

"Good morning. Would you like a table?" the hostess asked, a broad smile on her face and a chipper attitude to match.

"No, thanks. I see my friend over there. I think I'll join him." Sally prayed he wouldn't say no to company, or she'd have a hard time explaining her change in request.

"Enjoy your breakfast then." The server moved off, leaving Sally to make her way across the room.

"Mind if I join you?" she asked as he glanced up at her, a surprised expression on his face.

"Of course not. I would love the company. Surprised, but still good." He started to rise.

"No, no. Sit down." She liked that he was chivalrous, but there was no reason to stand on circumspect given the situation. Especially considering what she was about to do.

Randy took a sip of coffee and leaned back in his seat, his gaze fixated on her. "So what brings you to my corner of the world?" he asked.

"I wanted to apologize." Leading with sugar was a good idea, given her sour disposition since they'd first met.

The server approached. "Coffee, ma'am?"

"Yes, please," Sally said as the woman topped off Randy's mug.

"And for breakfast? Have you heard about the special?"

"Kyle told me, and I definitely want to try the avocado eggs. Thanks."

"It's one of the local favorites." The woman jotted down some notes on her pad.

"Apologize?" Randy asked as the server moved away.

"Yes. You were trying to help me yesterday, and I let my pride get in the way. If you're skiing today, I would love to accept your offer if it's still open." No one would expect Sally Castle to be getting lessons in the small town of Cedar Grove, Vermont. Not when some of the finest ski resorts in the world were available for her to use.

"This is quite a reversal, but I'm game. I'm giving myself until after the holidays to have some fun and enjoy life. Then I need to figure out my next step with regards to the military. So until then, I'm all yours for as long as you're in town."

All hers. No one had ever been all hers. It was a dangerous line of thinking, but if Sally did have an *all hers*, she would want the guy to be just like Randy. "Spoken like a true gentleman. I'm not sure how long I'll be in town, but it sounds like we have a deal." She reached out to shake his hand.

Randy reciprocated, holding on a second or two longer as he gazed deeply into her eyes. She glanced away, not wanting him to see too much, or worse, the real Sally. "I didn't know you wore glasses."

"Sometimes. The glasses are progressives, and I use them when I need to read. Like for the small print on a menu. Not much use for them out on the slopes." She needed to stop rambling.

"I see. How long have you been skiing?" Randy asked, making small talk.

"Long enough to be better than I am to-day." She evaded his question smoothly and applauded herself for the quick response. Lying wasn't her thing and she was already living a big one...no matter how temporary. "What about you?"

"I grew up here. With a course this close, I started skiing when I was ten, but then when I got out of high school and joined the military, there was no skiing. So I'm more than a little rusty but do remember a lot of what I learned. It's coming back to me."

Sally smiled, seizing the opportunity to set the record straight. *Sort of.* "Good. If we stick together, maybe we can both get back on our feet. I mean...you can get back your groove, and I can find my ski legs." She laughed, trying to cover her mistake.

"So what brought you to Cedar Grove besides skiing? Or is this strictly a vacation?"

She hadn't planned on playing twenty questions. "Business. Sort of. Business and pleasure, really. I wanted to get in some skiing."

"What sort of business?" Randy asked.

She searched her brain for a reasonable but true answer. "I'm in the sports industry. Just not at the top of my game right now and needed some recharge time."

"Now that I can totally understand. It's not unlike me and the military. My best friend was killed in action. He was getting out of the military and wanted something more for his life. Except it never happened. It's what prompted me to take an extended leave and sort out my next move before the opportunity to make a change is gone."

Randy's entire demeanor had grown pensive.

"I'm sorry. What happened? If you don't mind me asking, that is." She wished there was something she could say or do to ease the pain of losing his friend. But she also knew from experience that sometimes it was just a matter of letting someone talk about the person. The ability to bring them back to life, even if only in their memories.

"I don't mind. Ben was Misty's original owner. My buddy was engaged, and when he was killed, it devastated his fiancée. She is allergic to dogs, and Ben was trying to find a new home for the dog. She'd been staying with his grandparents, who were getting on up there in years. So before he died, I promised Ben to take care of Misty and find her a good home. But I'm not sure I want to let her go, so I haven't even started looking. I feel like I have ties to something that needs me as much as I need them for the first time. And she's such a great dog. You should meet her," Randy added, a light smile back in place.

He was a complex man with a huge heart, something she'd do well not to ignore. "I'd love to meet Misty. I've always wanted a dog, but it was never in the game plan."

Randy laughed. "Last time I checked, you're an adult. Guess you can do what you want now."

Sally disagreed. But then Randy didn't know the truth, something she was tempted to tell him after everything he'd shared. "You would think., but it's not as easy as you make it sound. There are things to consider." *Don't do it.*

"Such as?" he asked.

Sally shrugged. "It's complicated. I'd rather hear about you. Are you leaning in one direction or the other at this point about the military?"

"Honestly, I'm not sure what I'm doing besides exploring my options. The only thing I do know for certain is that I'm tired of traveling. My entire childhood was spent moving around from base to base all over the world as a military brat. Then I somewhat followed in my father's footsteps and joined the Army and have had to move around my entire adult life. It's exhausting. What if Ben was onto something with the whole idea of love, marriage, family, and a house—the American dream right down to the white-picket-fence?"

Sally shook her head. "It sounds lovely, but I can't believe I'm hearing a guy say it."

"I'm simply tired of never settling down in one place. What's wrong with stability and routine?" Randy asked, quirking one eyebrow up in question.

"Nothing. Absolutely nothing." It was the same thing she craved time and time again, but as of yet, the reality of the concept remained allusive. She always labeled the image as an after-her-career goal. The question was, when would that be? Now? A year from now? Or five years?

She'd been skiing, training, practicing, and competing since she was eight. Nineteen years later and she was tired of it. All of it. The hotels. The traveling. The circuit. But so much had been invested in making it as far as she did. There was no way she could give less than 110% to her father, the man who sacrificed everything for Sally to follow her dreams.

Except now, she could not even give 75%, much less go over and above. And she was in hiding from her father. Life had taken an ugly twist, and it was up to Sally to figure out her next move.

They ate their breakfast, Sally fielding his questions like an expert dodgeball player. Randy Granger was one of the nice guys—not to mention, a very handsome guy. One she might even be able to count as a friend when this charade was over. Provided, of course, he forgave her little white lies.

Okay...big white lies.

"I told you I was on to something," Chloe said, *pointing at the couple seated at the table in the corner of the bistro.*

"That you did, my dear. What do you think we should do? Or do we leave these two alone to figure it out?" Captain Tremont asked.

"Where's the adventure in that?" She laughed, taking him by the arm. "We're matchmakers, not watchers. But I'll think of a plan. She's hiding something, and I wish I could figure out what it is and why. Perhaps we should check her room to see if there are any clues."

"Even if I were to disagree, you'd do it anyway. You are one determined woman when it comes to getting your way."

"One determined ghost. And don't you forget it, Captain Tremont. I waited over two hundred years for you, so I think I can handle something like this in a matter of days. Child's play," she quipped.

The captain shook his head and laughed. "Just save me time for a dance, sweet lady."

"Always, Captain. Forever and always."

Chapter Six

♥

Randy couldn't help but notice Sally's aversion to give details about her life. The vagueness served to confirm something was wrong, but at this point, she wasn't willing to share. At best, he could be her friend while in town and see how it all played out. Not to mention, he was thrilled at her change of heart, and they were going to ski together.

It's not like he was an expert by any means, but he would do his best to impart some words of wisdom. Sally was a natural on skis, and most of her problem was loosening up and trusting herself. Something he could rectify if he made their outing fun.

He drove them to the ski resort on the outskirts of town, lucking out when they scored a parking spot close to the lodge. "I think we should warm up first."

"Sounds good to me. I'm a bit stiff from yesterday." Sally rubbed her calf muscles as if to prove her point.

She had only done one run and then left. Unless, of course, she had come back and he wasn't aware of it. Randy wondered if nerves played a part in her answer. "You know, it might be easier to go over some of the mechanics in slow motion. Over on Bear Run," he added to clarify.

Sally shot him a derisive glance, one eyebrow quirked up. "The bunny trail?"

"I hardly think the bunnies are skiing," he teased. "A green trail would make it easier for you to gain confidence."

She mulled over his suggestion, glancing back and forth between the two slopes. "Fine. Maybe you're right," she said, letting out a deep breath.

They eased their way to the chairlift, making sure none of the children from the ski school ran into them. Then, when it was their turn, they hopped on, making it look easy.

"Don't worry, I remember how to get off this thing." Randy winked.

"Good. I'm not sure I could take another bulldozing. I still can't believe I agreed to let the man who couldn't do a proper exit from a chairlift teach me anything about skiing. You must have addled my brain in the fall." Sally's teasing smile brightened his day considerably.

"Maybe so, but you did agree. And now, I've got a skiing partner for the day. One who manages to bring laughter to any situation. How can I go wrong?"

"If you laugh at me, so help me..." Sally swatted his arm.

"Not at you. Us. Fun." He pulled up his phone. "Smile for the camera," Randy said, wanting to capture the moment.

"No pictures." Sally held up her hand to block her face as she shook her head.

"Camera shy? That's not something I would have guessed." But it went along with his theory she was in hiding. The question was—from who or what? The idea didn't settle well with him, and his protective mode rose another notch.

"Yes. Please don't take pictures. That's all I'm asking."

Randy shrugged. "Fine." He lowered his phone. "I love to capture memories in pictures, but I guess this is one for the memory banks."

They arrived at the top and exited smoothly. They moved to the bunny trail as several children barreled past them, others with instructors and going super slow. The first-timers were easy to spot as they practiced the pizza wedges. Unfortunately, they were also the beginners you wanted to avoid.

Having never instructed anyone before, he realized he should start from the basics to make sure Sally had a good grasp of the mechanics. "Let's start with the pizza wedge I mentioned yesterday. I'm sure you can do them, but I want to see how comfortable you are when you pick up speed. You have to trust the process and know you'll stop if you do this one easy move."

Sally frowned, but just as quickly it vanished. "I thought we were here to ski—not eat," she teased.

It was a shame her goggles hid most of her face because the eyes were always more telling. "That's the pizza wedge," Randy said, pointing at several other kids practicing the move. "Yesterday, you had great moves, but honestly, I felt as though you were afraid to go faster. Want to try?"

"Sure thing. Pizza to the left, pizza to the right, pizza all the way home." She grinned.

It would seem she intended to use humor to cover her fear of going fast. "I think you're a bit confused on the songs and rhymes, but yes, something like that." Randy was all for making this fun, especially since it was Sally, and spending time with her was becoming increasingly important.

Sally started down the hill, slow at first and picking up speed. She wedged her skis and slowed, then stopped, turned, and nodded back up at him. Randy followed, passing her before coming to a stop to watch. She pushed off and started down the hill, gaining speed. Lots of speed.

Was she out of control? Did he push her too far, too soon? Randy raced after her, worried how the run would end. Crashing into the nets wasn't his idea of fun for anyone, especially not a skier learning to trust herself.

"Pizza," he yelled as loud as he could. It was like talking to a wall for all she would have been able to hear him.

She was almost to the bottom. Randy sucked in a deep breath waiting for the inevitable crash at the speed she'd mustered on the way down. Someone forgot to teach her that straight down was never good. That would be their next lesson...*if* there was a next lesson.

At the last second, Sally came to an incredible stop, digging in the edges of her skis and sending snow flying to the side. She turned to face him, hands in the air as if exhilarated by what she'd just done. Granted, it was a bunny slope, but in his eyes, it was lunacy. And Sally had enjoyed it, proving she was a natural at skiing, just as he expected. It all came down to trusting her instincts. Randy came to a stop next to her, still amazed she hadn't crashed.

"Did you see me?" she asked, her enthusiasm contagious. "That felt so good."

"You did awesome. Where'd you learn to stop like that? You had me worried, not going to lie," Randy said, pulling off his goggles to get a better look at his crazy student.

"I never said I couldn't ski. I've had some lessons, just not a lot of practice lately. We need to do that again," she said, sounding like a child on Christmas morning.

"Sure thing. But we need to talk about traversing from side to side. It helps you to cut your way down the slope under control and safely. You could have been seriously hurt if you'd crashed." Watching her career down the mountain out of control had about given him a heart attack, and he wasn't looking for a repeat performance.

Sally flinched, her radiant smile dissipating. "But I didn't crash." She shook her head, her brow furrowed. "The truth is, I had more fun than I would have thought possible. So lighten up, Mr. Ski Instructor."

She was right. Randy wanted her to have fun, hoping to alleviate her fears. Apparently, it worked, maybe too well. "Good. Let's do this then." She was clearly an adrenaline junkie, and Sally would get bored with him in no time at all if he insisted on her using common-sense caution. Sometimes people had to learn from their mistakes.

They got in line and rode to the top, Sally showing more confidence as she looked around, pointing out various skiers who had good form. It was interesting that she seemed to know so much about the sport for a novice. But then TV had brought the Olympics, and the World Cup to everyone's living room. The announcers always did a great job breaking down the mechanics and explaining what they saw as professional skiers careened down a mountain.

At the top, they exited the lift. Instead of heading for the bunny trail again, Sally turned to the Glades. She paused at the top, rubbing her left leg vigorously. The dangers multiplied on the blue trails if one got out of control like Sally had done on the earlier run. "Maybe we should do the green again?" Randy said, wondering if the stop she'd made had put undue stress on some of her leg muscles and were overly tight now as a result. It would be easy to pull a muscle if that was the case.

"No way. Don't be a spoilsport. You wanted to do this yesterday. I was still stiff and sore and mentally not ready. But now, things are different. Come on," she said, leading the way and giving him no choice but to follow.

"Okay, then." At the trailhead, he stopped next to her. "Listen, going straight down a hill is dangerous at best, and how skiers get hurt. You really need to traverse the slope to help slow things down a bit. In skiing, it's all about control if you don't want to become a rolling snowball down the slope," he teased.

"You're right. Being a rolling snowball is no fun, and I've been one before so I should know. But the trick is, you're not supposed to become one in the first place," Sally shot back at him.

It was the most relaxed he'd seen her since he first knocked her down. Her sweet laughter and smile were fresh and something a man could get used to. "Crashing at the bottom wouldn't be much fun either. How about you follow my lead this time?"

"Sure thing, Mr. Ski Instructor." Her grin was enough for him to know her acquiescence wasn't a sure thing.

Randy led the way, and surprisingly, Sally followed. Glancing back, he was impressed at how quickly she picked up on the control pointers and used them to her advantage. He came to a stop on the side by the tree line, wanting to watch her for a moment.

Her natural abilities were shining through, better than even he could have imagined. She came to a stop next to him and pulled off her goggles, something she rarely did.

"That was fun. Slow—but fun." She laughed.

"That wasn't even close to slow. I knew you wouldn't hold back if I dialed our speed down too much." He chuckled, loving this fresh and carefree side of Sally.

"I've seen you go faster, mister. Race you to the bottom," she called out, adjusting her goggles back into place.

"I'm not sure that's a good idea. Why don't we—"

"Afraid to lose?" Sally quipped before taking off down the hill.

Straight down. Left with no choice but to follow, Randy took off after her. But there was no way he was going down the line she'd taken. Once again, he was left to watch and wait anxiously to see what happened. And once again, she not only managed to make it to the bottom, but she executed an amazingly perfect stop.

Beginner's luck? Hardly. Sally was clearly far better at skiing than she had let on. Which then left the question,...why not tell him?

"You win," he said, drawing close to her at the bottom. "That was a crazy stunt to pull. The green trail was bad enough, but this?" He pointed back up the hill. "Is there something you're not telling me? Because I think you ski better than you let on."

Sally's smile faded. "I ski. I'm just not confident right now. It was you who assumed I couldn't ski and offered me lessons."

She was right...he had assumed. "Your confidence looks just fine to me."

"For now, thanks to you. I can't begin to tell you how much I needed this." She nodded, rubbing at her knee and calf again.

Her comment stunned him, more so because he couldn't imagine how he had played a role in helping her. It's not like Randy even knew what he was helping with. There was so much more going on than she let on, but he wouldn't press. Not yet. "Muscles sore?" he asked, willing to let the matter drop.

She shrugged. "You could say that. How about a short break, and then we do this run again?"

"Sure thing. But I'm thinking I can forget giving you lessons," Randy added with a grin.

"Probably." Her teasing smile warmed his heart as well as her laughter.

Randy was looking forward to what the rest of the day would bring because Sally was growing on him in ways he hadn't counted on.

They headed for the lodge. Sally replaced her goggles with glasses and pulled her hat down low. Once again, glancing around as if searching or hiding...he just wished he knew which. *And why.*

Chapter Seven

♥

SINCE THE ACCIDENT, THIS was by far the best day for Sally. No doctors. No training. No calisthenics. No timings. And no coach. Just fun. It had been even longer since before the accident that she enjoyed skiing simply for pure enjoyment. And Randy was a big part of why the day turned out the way it did. He had no clue who she was, and he'd gone to such sweet pains to help her.

Natural instinct had kicked in once Sally started to shake not only any deep-seated fears but once her leg muscles began functioning in a way they were used to. Lack of use had only made the injuries hurt worse, and rebuilding tissue and strength were an integral part of her healing. She wouldn't set any records, and her skiing would be considered subpar at best by her doctor, trainer, and her father.

But it was enough for Sally. Which was why she wanted to do this part of the rehab on her own—without interference.

It was freeing to be out on the slopes, not a care in the world, and to share the experience with someone like Randy. Someone who enjoyed skiing with her and hanging out together for no other reason than he wanted to. Of course, she had to be careful not to lead him into thinking their friendship would go any further, but today was something she needed. *Desperately.*

They finished the last run and headed for the car. "That was a blast," Sally said, falling in step beside Randy. A blast she would pay for tonight with aches and pains, but all worthwhile at the moment.

"I agree. You're fearless out there. After a while, I enjoyed watching you ski. But at first, I was as nervous as a parakeet in a cat cage. You certainly got your confidence quickly, and after that, you were rock solid."

"Good instructor," she teased. Keeping the inexperienced persona had been a lost cause with the lure of the slope calling her name, but she'd settled for the next best thing—experienced amateur. Sally had stuck close to Randy all day, just two friends skiing together.

Randy shook his head. "We both know better than that. You're a natural at this. You had all the moves; you just needed to have fun. Something you certainly showed me how to do after a while. So thank you. Today was special because it was shared with you."

"Thank you. Trust me, I needed it as much as you did. We'll call it even," Sally offered, smiling up at him. *Special.* It wasn't a word she'd heard often in regard to herself as a person rather than her abilities as a skier. A distinction that over the years began to mean more to her.

The problem wasn't just physical—it was also mental. Everyone expected so much from her. And people like her father had given so much of themselves to see her succeed. Except now, she wasn't sure she wanted to keep doing this. Wasn't there more to life?

But how did one say stop, not without hurting those who had helped get her where she was in the first place? The last thing she wanted to do was let her father down. It was these types of questions she'd asked herself over the past two years. Questions she still didn't have answers to.

Randy unlocked the truck, and they loaded their gear. He opened the passenger door and helped her inside. "Listen, I know this is sort of sudden, and I know we got off to a rocky start, but—"

"Snowy," Sally corrected.

"What?" he asked, the wrinkles across his forehead deepening.

"A snowy start." She grinned. "As in me in the snow, thanks to you." It was fun to tease him, especially since he'd gone to so much trouble to apologize.

Understanding hit him instantly. "That's true. I keep hoping you'll let it slide."

"I did. Right onto my keister." She laughed, slapping him lightly on the arm.

"Enough." Randy groaned.

"So, what were you going to say?" Sally would let him off the hook for now but reserved the right to use their introductory fiasco against him whenever she saw fit.

"I was wondering if you'd have dinner with me. Cade's Tavern is a nice place in town."

A date? She hadn't seen the invitation coming, and she really wanted to say yes. Sally shook her head. "I can't." It was far too public and too close to the ski resort where avid skiers would likely be found for après ski and dinner.

His smile faded. "I see. Okay, then. Just thought it would be nice after the day we shared." Randy seemed a little put out by her rejection.

It wasn't him…it was her. The typical line for rejection. The problem was, she didn't want the day to end either. Maybe if she was careful. *No. Foolish was a better word.* "I changed my mind. I'd love to go." She wished now she had dyed her hair. It would have been so much easier. So far, she hadn't been recognized at the slopes, so perhaps her luck would continue. Because until it ran out, she intended to make good use of her freedom. Do things she hadn't been able to do in forever. Like, go on a date with a man. A real date. Not a photo op or any other professional reason. This was personal.

"Really? That's awesome. They have the most mouth-watering, delicious baby back ribs you could imagine. And then maybe one night we could go to Angela's over in Willow Springs. I heard my sister talking about the place the other day, so I know they're still open. They had incredible grilled steaks if I remember correctly," Randy said, moving into a whole new territory.

Almost as if he was nervous? And if he was, why? "Whoa. Slow down. I only agreed to tonight. One date. Don't get ahead of yourself, mister."

"Well, now, you've gone and made that almost impossible. You just called our evening a date." Randy grinned. He drove back to the Crestfield Inn and parked, coming around to hold her door open.

"Thank you," Sally said, taking his hand as he helped her out of the truck. Randy was a true gentleman.

One who could be trusted. The idea came to her out of nowhere. Trust wasn't something she gave lightly, and there was too much at stake. She'd tell him the truth at some point, just not yet. For now, she just wanted to be Sally Chastain. Average skier. Average person. Average everything.

They both headed up the stairs to the second floor.

Randy paused at the top. "How long do you need to get ready? It's casual, so you don't really need to change."

"In that case, let me drop off my gear, freshen up a bit, and I'm ready. Say ten minutes?"

"Sounds good to me. A woman who can be ready in less than ten is a rare treat indeed."

In reality, less than ten wasn't typical for Sally. Not when one had to consider dozens of cameras always on you, waiting for her to make a mistake. The same people who were there to celebrate her wins. Their focus was a story...good or bad. "Glad I could be so accommodating." She grinned. "I'll meet you in the lobby." Going into her room, she put her gear in the corner and out of the way. She then scurried to the bathroom to see what needed to be done to get ready, hoping she hadn't overcommitted.

It turned out to be more like twelve minutes, but freshening up included touching up her makeup, changing into a fresh blouse and jeans. And rubbing in some of her special anti-inflammatory cream hoping to ward off the pain. She started to put her hair in a bun but a part of her wanted a softer, more feminine look and she couldn't do it. Instead, she went with just the glasses, hoping it would be enough. Well, the glasses and a dark corner table in the restaurant.

"You look gorgeous," Randy said when she made her way into the lobby. He leaned forward and kissed her cheek.

Just like an actual date. The kiss had caught Sally off guard. But more surprising was the rush of pleasure from the tenderness in which it was delivered. She was more than a little flattered by his attention, especially given his sincerity level rang true. "Thank you. I see I'm not the only one who changed for the occasion. I love the blue of that sweater on you. It's a perfect match to your eyes."

Randy chuckled. "Not exactly what I thought when I picked it out at the store. More like, I need something other than military green. And it was on sale."

"Good point." Sally smiled as he helped her put on her jacket.

They walked the short distance to Cade's Tavern. Randy held the door open, allowing her to enter first. Country music played on a jukebox in the corner, several couples on the dance floor. All around her, people were having fun, eating dinner, and socializing. And more than likely, none of them had to get up at four in the morning to start a day of intense training that would last all day.

But then, neither did she. Which is precisely why Sally wanted to make the most of this opportunity.

Randy led her to an open booth by the front window.

"*Ummm*, do you mind if we sit at that one, please?" she said, pointing to a booth in the far back corner. It looks cozier." *And private.*

"Fine by me. Cozy it is." They moved to the booth and slid in on opposite sides of each other.

It wasn't long before the server arrived. Sally was more than happy to let Randy place the order for the rib basket special, hoping his claim of mouth-watering deliciousness was accurate. And she was looking forward to getting messy and no one around to care.

"Seeing as we are officially on a cozy date now, I think it's time I found out more about you. For starters, may I ask how long you're in town for?" Randy asked, jumping right into the get-to-know-you stage after the server left.

"Honestly, I don't know. I'm hoping I'll be here at least a few more days, but at best, it's day to day. Why?" It was a stupid question to ask, and in hindsight, one she wished had a retract button.

"I'm enjoying my time with you, and like I said, it's needed after the seriousness of military life for ten years." Randy reached out and took her hand, his thumb grazing over her skin.

"I enjoyed today also. And I don't mind spending time together while I'm here, but that's where you and I end. I don't want to mislead you. What I really need is a friend, and I'd like to count you amongst them." Sally was trusting him with as much of the truth as was possible at this point. She took a sip of water to hide her nervousness as she waited for his answer.

He released her hand. "Friends, it is." Randy shot her a smile that could melt a woman's heart if she was so inclined. "For as long as you're here. Just promise me there's no one special back home waiting for you that might get upset we're on a date."

A question she could answer with total honesty. "There's no boyfriend or husband if that's what you're asking." Sally grinned, wanting to put him at ease.

Randy nodded. "Well that's good news. So where's home for you, and is that where you're headed after this?"

"I live in Vail. And yes, when my hiatus is over, I'll head back home."

Randy frowned. "I thought you were working here?"

Oops. Sally had told him that. "I am, in a way. I told you I was here to ski and on business." Skiing was her business so technically it was true. "Tell me about you. You said you have family here."

He leaned back in his seat, his gaze somewhat disconcerting. "I do. After my dad retired, they moved us here. It's where she grew up. My dad passed away not long after that. I think even then I started to wonder about my life choices because it seemed as though he missed out on so much family time. And before you know it, he was gone. Just like Ben in a way. Only Ben never even managed to start the family he wanted. I mean, serving your country is an honorable thing to do, and I've done it wholeheartedly, but I wonder what else there is in life. And then there's my sister. She has a happy marriage, a baby on the way, a place to call home. Stability. She's always telling me life in Cedar Grove is an adventure if you have the right person to share it with. I'm beginning to see things her way."

"Still going with the pregnant sister story, are you?" Sally teased. "I was sure that was totally made up. Your sister sounds like a lovely person."

Randy ran a hand through his hair and nodded. "Scout's honor, she's pregnant."

"Were you ever a scout?"

"No, but still." He laughed, crossing his heart with an x.

Randy was down to earth and not afraid to say what was on his mind. And she liked that he was a family man or wanted to be one anyway. He'd make someone a wonderful husband one day. Dedication was a strong character trait and one not easily found in the trappings of today's free-spirited world. "Are you upset your mother asked you to stay at the inn? I can't imagine just getting home and then being asked to leave. It doesn't seem right to me, but then I'm not exactly an expert on family and holiday protocol."

Randy shrugged. "Not at all. Christmas at my house can be overwhelming. It's a big deal. The house is fully decorated. The baking and cooking that goes on will easily add ten pounds if you're not careful. And the singing...carols galore. My aunt and uncle are the same way, so it's a house full of Christmas cheer."

"Sounds wonderful." Nothing like the Christmas's Sally experienced after her mother died. Those were extra practice days now. In hindsight, it was probably an easier way for her and her father to avoid painful memories. Now, Sally wasn't so sure it had been good for her emotional health. And now, Christmas was just around the corner again, and this year she'd be back in Vail celebrating at home in a house that wouldn't even be decorated. Somehow, the idea seemed more depressing than ever.

On the other hand, the spirit of Christmas 'present' still had the potential to be different. Christmas spirit was alive and well in Cedar Grove, and if she stayed here instead of returning home, it was hers for the taking. It was too tempting to pass up, even if it was only temporary. "You asked me earlier how long I was in town for and I told you not long. Days at best. But I've changed my mind. I will stay in town for as long as I possibly can, but at some point, just know I will have to go home. How's that for compromise?" It was more a matter of promising to stay until someone recognized her and she was forced to return to reality, but she wouldn't share that part of the equation.

"Till after Christmas?" he asked, pushing for something more specific.

Something Sally wanted more than he did most likely. "I'd like that. A lot. It might even give me some time to give *you* pointers in skiing," she teased, enjoying the back-and-forth camaraderie they shared.

"Now that's rich. The student giving the instructor lessons. I think your lack of fear has increased your boldness, and it knows no bounds." Randy sat back, his grin crinkling the sides of his deep blue eyes.

"Maybe. Guess you'll have to find out on the slopes tomorrow."

"Another date?" he asked.

Sally nodded. "Sounds that way. A date with destiny."

Randy seemed surprised by her answer. No more so than she was herself. Of course, she hadn't meant it the way it sounded.

Destiny on the slopes...not life.

"I like the sound of that." Randy winked, letting the comment slide, for the most part, much to her relief.

Dinner was served and discussions were dialed back to a slower speed as they ate, the promise of excellent food not an empty claim by any means. The baby back ribs were coated in a tangy-sweet sauce that left her craving more. Not to mention the crispy French fries she dipped in the same sauce, not caring one whit about the extra calories. At this point, she'd stopped counting.

It was a night she wouldn't soon forget. A couple of times she almost suggested dancing but warred with not wanting to give Randy the wrong impression. Friends danced, but sometimes, she herself was having a hard time distinguishing the friend line.

Sally yawned, one glass of wine enough to make her sleepy. Alcohol was another no-no on a professional athlete's diet. Or at least on her father's structured regime. She had learned a long time ago it was easier to agree with him—on everything. It was also why she disappeared without telling him. Freedom, if only for a short time, sounded like heaven.

"Sounds like you're tired. We should head back to the inn, especially if you want to be in top form tomorrow."

She nodded. "I am. And thank you. This was amazing. I'm going to run to the ladies' room first if you don't mind." It had been a long day, and she would need a good soak in the tub to ease the stiffness out of her muscles. Not to mention a healthy dose of the anti-inflammatory muscle cream she used daily.

"Sure thing. I'll settle up with the server." He reached for the bill the woman had dropped off.

This was the awkward part. "Let me get you my credit card—"

"Nonsense. My date and I pay. Not another word," Randy insisted, holding the tab out of her reach.

Which was a good thing considering she hadn't given thought to the fact her credit cards were all in the name of Sally Castle. The only reason the Crestfield Inn didn't know who she was is that Jessica had paid for the stay.

"Well, okay then. Thank you," Sally said before moving off to go to the bathroom.

She had to wait in line a few minutes and did her best pretending to look at the photos on the wall. It was the easiest way for no one to get a good look at her. And after her turn, she headed back into the hall and into the main area.

A woman stood, moving in front of Sally and blocking her path, the woman laying one hand on Sally's arm. "Aren't you Sally Castle?" the woman asked, her eyes aglow with excitement.

Sally drew back, stunned. "Flattering, but no. I'm sorry." She delivered the response hoping it would have the desired effect.

The woman didn't move as if not able to believe she'd been wrong.

Sally removed the woman's hand and walked away, unwilling to give anyone else a chance to connect the dots and start pulling up photos for comparison. She may have just promised Randy she'd stick around until after Christmas, but it would seem her promise might have been a little premature and that her days were numbered here in this peaceful little town.

Chapter Eight

♥

THE FLAMBOYANTLY DRESSED WOMAN engaged in conversation with Sally captured Randy's interest, especially when Sally walked away briskly. "What was that all about?" he asked when she approached.

"Oh, nothing. Just a case of mistaken identity," Sally answered, her voice a little too nonchalant for his satisfaction.

Especially given the tension radiating from her...a tension that hadn't been there when she left to go freshen up at the ladies room. "Get that often?" he teased, trying to lighten the mood.

"You'd be surprised," Sally said, gazing at him as if deep in thought. But just as quickly, the expression disappeared with a barely visible shake of her head. If he hadn't been paying close attention, it would have been missed. "You ready to go?"

"Absolutely." Randy held out his hand, gesturing for her to go ahead of him.

He helped with her coat, and then holding open the door, he allowed his hand to drift to her waist to guide her outside. The change from a dry to icy surface could take a person unaware. Randy preferred not to repeat their introduction, leaving his hand there on the walk back to the inn.

The evening had brought many surprises, including the connection he felt with Sally. His interest in her seemed to multiply as they spent more time together, and with each tidbit he found out about her. The biggest surprise was her change of heart and decision to stay until after Christmas. Hope surged within in him that perhaps, she too was interested and felt the connection they shared.

"Are you cold?" he asked, holding out his scarf to wrap around her neck for added warmth.

"I'm okay, thanks. Do you need to take Misty out when we get back?"

It was sweet of her to think about the dog, another sign of her caring concern for others. "I do, but it can wait a bit if you want to join me by the fire for a glass of wine." He wasn't ready for the evening to end.

"Absolutely. The wine sounds nice, but truthfully, you had me at sitting by the fire. I'm so cold." She laughed, the sound beautiful and a good sign she'd fully recovered from the incident in the restaurant.

He held the door to the inn open for Sally, the fresh scent of pine, cinnamon, and apple greeting them as they stepped inside. Candles were lit. Soft Christmas music played.

"Thanks," she murmured.

He was disappointed to realize they weren't alone in the lobby. More so because the two guests were glued to the sports channel on a TV in the corner of the room—one he hadn't even noticed before. *So much for a romantic evening by the fire.*

Sally suddenly grabbed his arm and pulled him around, doubling over to grab her calf.

"What's wrong?" he asked, reaching out to steady her.

"It's my leg," she said, her voice louder than necessary. "It's cramping. Please, can you help me get upstairs," Sally pleaded, her expression one of anguish.

"Of course. Put your arm around my neck, and I'll support you. Can't have you falling on my watch," Randy tried for light-hearted humor, but it fell flat. It was like being on a roller-coaster with her, and at the time, left him reeling.

Sally grimaced, moaning as the pain intensified.

"Sorry, guess this isn't a teasing moment." Randy scooped her up in his arms and carried her up the stairs, her face buried against his shoulder. Protective feelings as he held her close.

"You can set me down now," Sally said when he reached her room.

"Are you sure? I can hold you while you unlock the door, and then I can carry you inside," he offered.

She shook her head. "No, I'm fine. The cramp has subsided."

The cramp might have, but Sally's tension hadn't. He did as she asked, intending to follow her inside to make sure she was okay.

"Thank you for tonight," Sally said, the dismissal in her voice unmistakable.

Any chance for a romantic evening disappeared because of a cramp. There was a first time for everything. "Okay, then. Are we still skiing tomorrow? We could meet for breakfast again and ride over together."

"*Ummm*. I'm not sure that's a good idea. I might need to rest a day or two. The cramps are a good indicator I may have overdone things today. I'm sorry. Goodnight." Sally closed the door, officially ending the evening.

Randy headed down the hall, making use of the opportunity to take Misty out for a potty walk. *At least the dog always seemed to enjoy his company.*

Sally breathed a sigh of relief as the door closed behind her. It had been a close call. Too close. Quick thinking brought on a fictitious cramp to keep Randy from hearing the news and stopping to give it a closer look. But it was also to keep the other guests from matching her image with the image on the screen. It wouldn't have taken long to connect the dots.

That was the second time today and more proof her time in Cedar Grove was limited. Where to next, she wasn't sure. But if she could stay ahead of her father's search, she would keep trying. She loved her father, but he'd controlled almost every aspect of her life since her mother's passing.

Granted, Sally had let him. But lately, the edge to succeed was missing. The accident may have ruined her career, but whether she returned or not, the downtime was just what she needed. So the accident was both a blessing and a curse.

Three strikes and Sally would flee the area, not at all ready to face the media. Or her father. Coach Castle wouldn't approve of her recent choices. And Sally didn't want to hear the disapproval in her father's voice as he lectured her on the life of a professional athlete.

Sally's last Christmas with both parents, Santa had brought her a pair of skis. It was then that Sally had declared she wanted to be just like Peekaboo Street. And it was her mother who had been adamant that one day, Sally would stand on the highest podium at the Olympics and receive a gold medal.

And it was that memory that had driven Sally over the years to push herself and to prove her mother right. But Sally had done that and more. Now she wanted something else for her life. The problem was her father would never understand, and the last thing she wanted to do was disappoint him.

She'd agree to spend the Christmas holidays in Cedar Grove, but at this point, there was next to no chance of that happening. Perhaps she had been too hasty in rejecting Randy's offer to ski tomorrow. If her time was limited, she should be making the most of it, not hiding out in her room. Randy enjoyed hanging out with her as a person. A friend. Not as a celebrity. Normal was looking pretty attractive right about now, especially when it came in the form of Randy Granger.

Sally glanced out the window and spotted Randy walking Misty. Her gaze followed them a way before returning to the nativity scene set up in the front yard. A gentle reminder of the joy, peace, and love of the holiday season. All things Sally could use more of in her life.

If she only knew how to find them—and hold on.

"Quit nudging me, my dear. I saw the same thing you saw. Trust me." Captain Tremont grinned.

"Well, usually, I must explain some of these things," Chloe teased, lacing her arm through his as they floated up the stairs to the attic.

"What's to not see? Our Sally is one and the same with the missing skier the news people are all trying to find."

"Exactly. And Sally saw the news on the television right before her cramp struck. So now we know what she is hiding and why she is here. The question is, how can we make her stay?" she asked.

Captain Tremont frowned. "That's your area of expertise."

"We've got to somehow get them to do more than ski and eat meals together because that's the area of her life she's running from...but what? If Sally's injuries are still a problem, it shouldn't be anything strenuous. Seems to me she's pushing herself kind of hard as it is. I've seen her limping when she thinks no one is watching."

"Randy is a local. What about something involving his family?" Captain Tremont asked.

Chloe shook her head, deep in thought. "We have no way to make anything like that happen. However, we can give nudges within the confines of the Crestfield Inn and gardens."

"The gardens are out this time of year. Nothing romantic about freezing." He grinned. "What about dancing?"

"That involves her legs, and there's only so much dancing one can do. There must be something," Chloe said, tapping the side of her face with her finger.

"What about the craft fair in town? There's a brochure about it in the lobby," Captain Tremont offered.

"Hmmm. You know, that might just work. But we have to move quickly and find a way to nudge them in that direction. I sense our time is

running out. If Sally gets spooked again, she'll high-tail it out of here."

"Spooked...huh?" He grinned.

"You know what I mean." Her own grin widened, matching the handsome captain. "And now, why don't you honor me with a dance, Captain Tremont?"

"I would love to, my dear."

Chapter Nine

♥

"COME ON, MISTY. YOU must be as cold as I am," Randy said, shivering in the chill of the evening air. He turned around and gave the leash a slight tug to let the dog know his intentions as well. They were still working on commands since Misty was "new to him," and she thought the new master needed some training.

Woof. Woof. The dog walked beside Randy, setting a brisker pace than they had on the way out. The two of them were definitely thinking alike. *Inside equated to warmth.*

Randy pulled open the door, waving at Kyle when he spotted him behind the counter. Talk about being committed to one's job, it seemed the man was always on duty.

"Oh, hey. I'm glad you're here," Kyle called out.

Randy turned back from the stairs and made his way to the counter. "What's up?"

"Your mother called, and she left a message. They wanted you to stop in for a bit this evening. Said they haven't seen you all day." Kyle pushed a note in his direction. "I was just about to put this in your mailbox."

"That sounds about right." Randy chuckled. "Heaven forbid if we didn't see each other for over twenty-four hours."

Misty pulled at the leash, intent on checking out something that caught her attention. Randy didn't see anything, but with a dog, there was no telling. *Woof.*

"Come on, girl, there's nothing there." Tail up, Misty continued to sniff the air, resisting his lead.

"Probably the potpourri. Maybe the dog is not a fan of cinnamon apple," Kyle teased.

Randy moved closer, wanting to pet the dog and regain her attention. Except when he moved, the slack line gave Misty room to jump forward, pulling him with her.

Woof. Woof. A stack of red flyers landed on the floor.

"No, Misty. Sit." The dog complied. "Stay," he added, just as Kyle came around the counter.

"Let me get those; it's no big deal," Kyle offered.

"My dog, my responsibility. But thanks." Randy leaned down and shoved them all back into a pile, stood, and replaced them on the table nearby. It was a stable oak end table and how Misty managed to knock them off in the first place was a conundrum. Turning to walk away, the words "craft fair" caught his attention. He stopped, picking up one of the flyers and reading it over.

"This any good?" Randy held up the flyer as he asked the question.

"The seventh annual. The fair gets bigger and bigger every year. The whole town is filled with Christmas spirit, and this just brings it home if you ask me. It's a not-to-miss event if you can help it," Kyle explained.

"Sounds like fun. I wonder if Miss Chastain would be interested in something like this? Randy wanted to make her time in town fun, and this would give them more time together than simply skiing down a mountain. And fun was something they both needed.

"Only one way to find out. Ask." Kyle grinned as he delivered the not-so-subtle hint.

Randy nodded. "You're right. I think I'll do just that. And then head to my parent's place. Thanks for the message."

"Anytime," Kyle said, reaching to answer the ringing phone.

Misty had stayed put like a good girl, her earlier reaction a thing of the past. What-ever bothered her before, she'd clearly lost interest. He folded the flyer and stuck it in his pocket, and then headed upstairs. At the top, Randy turned left and made his way to Sally's room.

Knock. Knock. It wasn't long before Sally opened the door.

"Randy? Is something wrong? I thought we…oh, here's the sweet baby I've been dying to meet." Sally started to kneel but changed her mind, sitting on the chair nearby instead.

Misty gave her a warm tongue-bath hello amidst peals of laughter from Sally. Randy considered Misty an excellent judge of character, and Sally had clearly passed.

She glanced up at him, still petting the dog. "So, what's up? Did I forget something?"

"No, no. Nothing like that. I'm headed to my folks at the moment, but I discovered this in the lobby." Randy pulled the flyer out of his pocket to hand it to her. "Since you're not up to skiing tomorrow, I wondered if you would want to go to the craft fair instead. Kyle says it's a not-to-miss event. What do you say? Any interest in going?"

Her eyes lit up, reminding him of a child at Christmas. "Yes," she said, not a trace of hesitation evident in her voice.

"Well, okay then. Judging by your response, I'm super glad I mentioned it."

"Me, too. Can we bring Misty?" she asked, still fawning over the dog.

Randy was almost a little jealous of the attention Misty was getting. Almost, but not quite, because more than anything, he liked seeing Sally's face lit up with joy. "I don't think that's such a good idea. It might be easier to drop her off at my mother's house first. Misty still gets a little overly excited in crowds."

Sally stood. "I know you've got to get going, but thanks for thinking of me and the fair. I'm looking forward to it."

Her response was genuine, and it made his heart do a little flip-flop. "Sure thing." Randy had the sudden inclination to kiss Sally. A case of nerves struck him like he was a schoolboy with his first crush.

"Good night," she said, heading back inside and closing the door.

He'd missed his chance to kiss Sally. But tomorrow was a new day, and he'd be more prepared to act on a moment.

By the time he reached his mother's place, he was kicking himself in the behind. A wise man would have asked her to come with him tonight. Although, perhaps it was best to put out feelers with the family and make sure they wouldn't do anything to embarrass him. Things like telling tales out of school or by doing any matchmaking business.

His love life was his own, and he was pretty sure he could manage it. Time would tell, but for now, this was a no-interference zone, especially as he already wanted to move his friendship with Sally into a relationship zone. *His family, on the other hand, might scare her off.*

"So who's the lucky lady, Randy?" his sister asked, not even letting him get his coat off before she started in with the teasing. Her husband sat on the arm of the couch, holding his very pregnant wife close, matching grins on their faces.

Randy shrugged. "No one you know."

"Oh, come on. Don't keep us hanging. Kyle said you were on a date. We want details, young man," his mother said, moving into the room with a tray of mugs steaming with hot chocolate.

"I'm not sixteen." He took one of the cups and moved to sit by the warmth of the fire, the crackling flames dancing an invitation.

His uncle shook his head. "Son, you're always a boy in your mother's eyes, and if you think any answer short of the truth is going to get them to stop, you aren't as smart as I thought you were."

Randy knew his uncle was right. Of course, there was an answer he could give that would satisfy them all, and it was worth a shot. "You'll get to see for yourself when we drop Misty by in the morning. Sally and I are going to the craft fair." He dropped the bomb and waited to see the ripple effect.

Stunned silence greeted him for all of five seconds.

"Well, then. I guess that says it all. We look forward to meeting your friend," his mother said, letting the matter drop.

"Well played, Randy. Well played," his uncle said, clapping him on the back.

"It was certainly worth a shot." Randy grinned.

No longer the center of attention, it gave him time to think about tomorrow, his anticipation growing with each hour that passed.

Chapter Ten

♥

FINDING THE RIGHT OUTFIT from the limited selection she had brought took Sally more time than she had planned to get ready. How often did a girl get to go on a date and have reason to get spruced up? Maybe for some girls, a lot...but for Sally...spruced up meant for a photoshoot or to impress an endorser. Something in short supply these past two months.

Knock. Knock.

She glanced at her watch. The man was definitely on time, something she valued highly. Pulling open the door, she was excited to see both the man and his beast. She gave Misty a hug, the spontaneity and excitement enough for her to share the same greeting to the dog's owner. "Good morning," she said, hoping he would be okay with her forward behavior.

"And good morning to you as well." He hugged her back, the slightest of hesitation letting her go giving Sally a boost of confidence. "I see you're ready to go."

"And then some. You have no idea. I'm always about work, and this is a rare opportunity for me." Dressed in jeans and a thick blue wool sweater, she would be comfortable and warm. Her fur-lined boots were also good for warmth, but they had the added bonus of being stylish to add to their attributes.

"Then let's go. It's only a few blocks from here to Liberty Park, but we still need to take the car to get Misty to my mom's place."

Sally ruffled Misty's fur, earning her more of the doggy licks. "Sounds good. Having a car at our disposal means I can buy more than I can carry." She grinned. Either way, there was a credit card waiting to be used. And if her time was almost up here...what did it matter? With everything done electronically, most places wouldn't see her card or her signature.

Ten minutes later, they arrived at his mother's house. The place was a big, old Victorian home, its landscaping inviting to all. Massive amounts of Christmas decorations were on display, turning the home into a winter wonderland. Not as bad as the Griswold family in *National Lampoons Christmas Vacation*...but more than most. In fact, they would undoubtedly win the most decorated house on the block if there was such a contest.

Her nerves grew taut as he pulled into the driveway. Up close, there was always a danger of being recognized. But, it was a risk she was willing to take. She'd already come too close to losing her anonymity, and the lure of spending the morning at a craft fair came at a premium.

"They won't bite. I promise," Randy teased, taking her by the hand and leading her up the walkway. Misty trotted up to the front porch automatically.

"That's comforting." Sally laughed, pulling her hat low over her head and wrapping the scarf around her face. What wasn't comforting was two women coming out of the house to meet her. Or maybe they were only here for Randy and the dog. One could hope. She took in a deep breath, not wanting to let it get to her. Act normal.

"Hey, everyone. I'd like you to meet Sally Chastain, a friend of mine," Randy said by way of introductions.

His mother stepped forward to hug her. "Call me Tracy, please. It's a pleasure to meet you, dear. My son has told us nothing about you, but I understand why he's keeping you a secret. You're very pretty and I'm sure my son is worried we will start pushing you two together."

The knots in her stomach unfurled, her welcome genuine. "Thank you, ma'am."

"And this is my daughter, Naomi. She's eight months pregnant and looking like she's going to explode," Tracy teased, wrapping an arm around her daughter. "But they tell me it's a healthy grandson, so that's what matters."

Naomi shook her head and frowned. "Mother. Stop, please. You're not helping my stress. It's nice to meet you, Sally. Can you come in and stay for a while? I'd love to have someone else to talk to."

Meeting Randy's very pregnant sister sealed the deal. Everything he had told her had been the truth. She was not only blown away but impressed. "It's nice to meet you all. I'm sorry, but we've got plans this morning. You're so fortunate to live in Cedar Grove. I've been enjoying the area, and the slopes are pretty awesome. I can't believe I haven't skied here before." She was doing the whole talking to hide your nerves thing, and she needed to shut up.

"Such a kind spirit. She's a keeper, Randy," his mother said, smiling.

A keeper? No. No. They were friends. She was leaving soon and giving these friendly people the wrong impression wasn't her plan. "We should head to the fair, Randy. Wouldn't want to miss out on any of the fun," she said, taking a few steps back. It was one thing to spend time with Randy, quite another to get his family involved and think they were an item.

Randy nodded. "Okay. Head for the truck and I'll be right there. I'm just going to take the dog inside and get her settled."

"It was nice meeting you all," Sally said, stepping off the porch.

"It was nice to meet you as well," his mother said.

Sally turned and headed back to the truck, leaving Randy to take care of Misty and say his goodbyes. Moments later, he was on the porch talking with his mother and sister. When all three suddenly turned and looked in her direction, Sally was fully aware of what it meant their conversation was about her. Had they recognized her? Was Randy about to call Sally out for her deceit?

He returned to the vehicle, a serious look on his face and she feared she was right.

"What was that all about?" she asked, wanting to know but almost afraid to find out.

Randy turned toward her, taking her hand in his. "The thing is, they want to know if you'd like to join us for dinner tonight. I totally get it if you don't, but they were pushing me to ask. I could beg out—"

"Yes." The word was out before Sally could stop it. So much for not involving the family. But when was the last time she enjoyed a family dinner? Not since she was eight and her mom died. The temptation was too strong...even if it wasn't her family.

"Are you sure? You honestly don't have to do this," Randy said, his thumb grazing her cheek tenderly.

"Yes, I'm sure," she said, eliminating her last chance to back out of the commitment. Yes, and heck yes, was a better answer. Her plan had been to enjoy hanging out with Randy until she left, but now, those plans simply included a few more people.

Sally couldn't help but wonder what it would be like if this were real—like he was actually her boyfriend. Or if this was her meeting the family and moving the relationship forward. It would be easy enough to pretend he was her boyfriend—but no, she needed to avoid imagining something that didn't exist. Wishful thinking didn't change who she was or the fact she was here using a fake name.

Relationships were a distraction to her goals and career. Always had been. Bobby was proof. But then that distraction had moved on without even bothering to visit her in the hospital, which left more than enough doubt in Sally's mind about her ability to pick a great guy.

Randy nodded, the corners of his eyes crinkling as he smiled his approval. "Then I guess it's dinner at my family's home. I'll let my mom know. I'm sure they will be all overjoyed. Just don't say I didn't warn you."

"Considering myself warned." Sally laughed. Seize the day. This was just the first time she applied the motto to something other than skiing in a long time.

Randy drove the short way to Liberty Park in the center of town and parked. "Hold on and let me get your door." He slid out of the driver's seat and came around the truck without bothering to wait for her response.

"Thank you," Sally said as he took her hand and helped her out. She'd forgotten what it felt like to be cherished. Once upon a time, Sally had felt that special connection with her mother and father. Since then, the people she hung out with were mostly centered on themselves and making their way to the top. Or they were at the top and trying to hold on. Something she was guilty of in a competitive world where few succeeded.

Sally couldn't help the surge of excitement racing through her as they made their way to the rows of tents. There were already a lot of people milling about. She pulled her wool scarf a little tighter around her neck and lower face and checked to make sure her hat and glasses were doing their job. Satisfied, she moved to the first tent, looking over the custom-made wooden toys.

"These are adorable," she said, picking up one of the train engines. I don't have anyone to buy one for, but I can't imagine a child not loving this."

"My sister's boy will most likely be one of those kids. In a few years, that is." Randy laughed.

She set the engine back on the display rack and moved to look at the game boards. "True. I'm sure there are some age limitations, but I'm not the person to chime in. I don't have much experience with children, even less with babies." Not much experience with games either, for that matter.

"Do you want kids of your own one day?" Randy asked, following her as she moved to the next booth.

Pregnancy and children didn't play into her world of never-ending training and competitions. "Never really thought of it." It's not like she woke up one day and didn't want them; it was just never an option as a professional athlete. Thinking about it would have been a dead-end street. But now? The question was in play. Even if she did return to competition, it wouldn't last. And then what?

Randy quirked an eyebrow and nodded. "Interesting. It's an unusual answer for a woman. So what do you think about? And what do you do for fun back in Colorado?"

She picked up a set of hand-painted wildlife coasters and held them up for inspection, loving the fox and the bear and how real they looked. "Like I said, my job requires that I monitor the sports industry-which includes a lot of travel. So there's not much time for fun—believe me." She wanted to give him more...but what if he connected the dots. Still, she trusted him, and he deserved the truth. Or maybe a slice of it. "My father coaches a skier, and where he goes, I go."

"So like a father-daughter business?"

Sally shrugged. "Sort of, yes. He runs the show." Addison Castle was a coach, manager, and travel agent all rolled into one, and last but not least, her father. "I've got to have these," she said, pulling out her credit card. "The artist did such an amazing job, and I love that they won't take up much room in my suitcase."

"As opposed to the carload you planned to buy before we arrived?" he teased.

"I can always have some stuff mailed home. I like to pick up fun local artisan crafts from my travels for around the house. It adds a unique and worldly quality."

"I see. So is the skier your father coaches, anyone I would recognize?" Randy asked while she paid the bill.

"I don't think so, considering you've been gone ten years. Not unless you followed the circuit while on deployment." Sally laughed, unwilling to make up a name and outright lie. Hedging was a much better way.

"Thank you." The woman smiled as she handed her the plastic bag with her purchases. "Merry Christmas."

"Merry Christmas to you," Sally said before moving off to the next tent, leaving Randy to follow. She was hoping for a change in subject.

The booth had a wide array of quilted potholders, most of them for Christmas. Picking up a potholder with Santa Claus on the front, she held it out toward Randy. "I should get this for you, Mr. Apology Pie," she teased.

"Laugh all you want, but you enjoyed my cooking. And Apology pie worked, seeing as you're here with me. No kitchen can have too many potholders, and one day I'll have a place of my own, and this potholder will make me think of you and our time here today. I like the idea." He winked.

Sally couldn't stop the rush of pleasure at his words. It was a dangerous game when emotions got involved in friendships, but darn if she could put an end to the flirtation. "Nice to hear you are serious about settling down. I was worried you might be that guy...you know...the one turning forty and still living at home. Wasn't there a movie about that?" She grinned.

"Not me. Not by a long shot. And if I decide to get out of the military in a few weeks, a house isn't far off. I love the idea of staying in one place."

"That settles it then. I'll take this," Sally said to the woman, handing her a five-dollar bill.

"Wonderful. I'll be right back with your change," the woman smiled and made her way to the cash box set up on a table toward the back.

"I wasn't seriously asking you to buy it for me," Randy said.

"I know. But you've been sweet to me and, well, you can consider it a thank you. For everything." Sally blushed.

"You're forgetting something very important. No serious chef would have a mismatched set of potholders. I'm sure the minimum is like three or four in a set. I mean, you can't have a Santa Claus without a Mrs. Claus. It wouldn't be right." The corners of his eyes crinkled, his grin widening.

"True. Who else would cook for Santa and keep him filling out his suit? Perhaps you should put potholders on your list for Santa." Sally vowed if she could catch a few minutes to herself, she'd be sure to come back and buy him a few more, including Mrs. Claus. Then, she could put it under the family Christmas tree tonight while she was at his house. Come Christmas morning, Randy would have an unexpected surprise.

"Thank you," the woman said, handing her the change and a plastic bag.

"I love that these are handmade. My mother made these in her spare time, and I think they add a special touch to anyone's kitchen. Merry Christmas," Sally said, ready to move to the next tent.

"Merry Christmas."

Five tents and two packages later, they stopped at a booth offering hot beverages. "Any interest in some hot chocolate?"

Randy asked as he stopped to read the menu.

She nodded. "Absolutely. A Christmas craft fair wouldn't be complete without one."

"Why don't you go find us a table, and I'll order?"

"Sounds like a plan." Sally looked around, spotted an empty picnic table, and moved to claim it.

It wasn't long before he returned with two mugs of hot chocolate, topped with whipped cream and green and red sprinkles. "Here you go," he said, holding one out to her.

"Those look delicious." She took one from him and raised it to her lips, sipping carefully so as not to get burned. "*Hmmm*. Now that's some serious hot chocolate."

"Don't let anyone hear you call it that." Randy chuckled. "Around here, when it's homemade, it's hot cocoa. Or so I was informed."

"I see. Good to know. Wouldn't want to be thrown out of Cedar Grove for insulting their best cocoa maker." Sally laughed, having more fun than she could remember. But then, everything with Randy was more fun, something she couldn't fail to notice.

Once they finished, it was on to more tents and watching some of the children play. The skating rink brought back another memory of her mother. Round and round she and her mother had skated, holding hands and laughing. Sally shoved the image aside, not wanting anything to spoil the day.

"Do you want to skate?" Randy asked, leading her closer to the rink.

"*Ummm*, not really. I don't know how," Sally said, skirting the issue.

"That's something we'll have to rectify, but perhaps another day. Let's go stand by the fire and warm our hands a bit. It looks like the kids are toasting marshmallows or something." Randy grinned.

"That sounds lovely." They moved to the giant bonfire but soon discovered there were more than marshmallows being cooked. Kids and adults alike were holding broomsticks over the fire, with something akin to a pastry of sorts on the end. Sally was intrigued and moved to stand next to a woman holding one of the sticks over the fire. "What is it you're making?"

"These are called broomsticks." The woman laughed and brought the end toward them for Sally to get a good look. "It's a crescent pastry wrapped around a greased pieced of tinfoil on the end of a broomstick. You toast it slowly until it slides off the end easily."

"And then what? Surely that doesn't taste good enough to warrant what you're doing?" Randy asked, getting into the learning curve.

"Of course not. When it's finished, you get to the good part. Picking a filling. There's like four kinds over on that table, and you scoop your favorite into the hole left by the stick. I think they have cherry, apple, peach, and strawberry."

"Like pie?" Sally asked, grinning at Randy. There was nothing wrong with more pie.

"Exactly," the woman said, testing hers again. It slid right off the end. "Time for me to add some strawberry filling. Here, take this," she said, handing them the broomstick. "Take a turn. The tinfoil squares are over there." She pointed at the table they'd walked by when they entered the area.

"How can two pie lovers say no?" Randy asked.

"We can't." Sally chuckled, determined to try everything. When they finished cooking the pastries, both chose peach pie filling, spooning the warm gooey liquid into the hole. Sally took a bite and the filling started to fall out. She licked it off the pastry before it fell to the ground. *"Hmmm,* this is so good. The hint of smoke adds to the peach flavor."

Randy took a second bite, nodding in agreement. "It's also messy." He took his napkin and dabbed at the corner of her mouth.

Standing this close, the intimacy of the moment wasn't lost on Sally. It was a tender and thoughtful gesture given by someone who cared. She was sure he wanted to kiss her, and Sally was sure she wanted him to as well.

Someone jostled them from behind and they moved apart...the moment over.

They continued to explore the entire park, and by the time she spotted Santa, she was more than ready to get in line, not wanting to miss any of the fun. "Let's do this," she said, pointing at the Santa's workshop area where kids were lined up with their parents waiting on their turn.

"Sure thing," he responded without the slightest hesitation. Randy was a guy who knew how to have fun and didn't care about image.

Something she always had to worry about—but not today.

When it was their turn, Santa's broad grin meant he was enjoying their fun as much as they were. Of course, Randy and Sally were too big to sit on the man's lap, but they were young enough to join in the Christmas spirit.

"*Ho, ho, ho*. What would you like for Christmas, little lady?" Santa asked.

"I would love a Candy Land game." She could feel her cheeks flush warm with the admission.

"And what about you, young man? What would you like for Christmas?"

"A firetruck with flashing lights and a siren." Randy grinned, his answer all in keeping with their merriment.

"What? No potholders?" Sally teased as she reminded him about her earlier comment.

Randy shook his head. "No. I'll stick with the firetruck. That way if there's a fire in my kitchen, I'll have a way to put it out."

The man had an answer for everything, his sense of humor on full display.

"*Ho, ho, ho.* Santa will see what he can do about getting you those presents, but only if you're on the good list."

"Always, Santa," Randy said, a glimmer of mischievousness in his eyes.

They moved behind the jolly old man and took a few selfies—something else Sally had changed her mind on when it came to Randy. When their turn was over they moved off to the next set of tents.

Sally admired the unique jewelry, picking up several pieces and trying to decide what she wanted. "Why don't you go ahead, and I'll catch up? There's nothing here to interest you, and I'd like to look a little closer."

Randy nodded. "Okay, sounds like a plan. I see some baby clothes just ahead, and I think I could pick something up for my soon-to-arrive nephew as a Christmas present."

"You're such a softie."

"Don't tell anyone," he said, winking before he walked away.

Sally turned back to the sales clerk. "These are gorgeous. What kind of stone is it?" The bright blues were intertwined with green and brown, reminding her of an abstract seascape painting.

The older woman's kindly smile reached her eyes. "Thank you, dear. They are Peruvian Opals. I have a niece that sends me the stones to make into jewelry. I'm from there originally, and it gives me a wonderful sense of peace. Like I'm working with a part of home I miss."

So the woman wasn't just the sales clerk, she was the designer. "What a lovely sentiment. And the craftsmanship of the silver is exquisite. I've never seen so much love go into the mount for a stone as the designs you've created. Do you ever wish you could go back? To Peru, that is?" Sally asked, holding up her favorite piece to the light for a better look.

"Oh, no. This is my new home. I met my husband not far from here while I was vacationing in the United States. We fell in love, got married, and we raised three daughters here. Now I've got six grandchildren. This is my home and my life. This is where my heart is."

The woman spoke with such passion that Sally couldn't help but respect her choices and her commitment. It couldn't have been easy giving everything up she once knew to start over, and yet she'd done it and never regretted the decision. "Wow. What a wonderful story."

"Love is a wonderful story, my dear. It's just a matter of finding the right person and then holding on with everything you have."

"I'll remember that." Sally held the pendant against her neckline, but her scarf was in the way. Not to mention, her glasses made it difficult to get the full depth of color. Glancing around, she didn't see anyone nearby. She unwound the scarf, unzipped her jacket, and removed her glasses before holding the pendant in place and viewing the loveliness through the large, round mirror on the case. It was perfect.

"Oh, my gosh, it's her," a young girl said, squealing with delight.

Sally spun around, instantly on alert. She pushed her glasses back into place for protection just as two girls rushed up.

"Please, Sally, please. We love you. Will you sign our...oh, what do we have for her to sign?" one girl said to the other, completely flummoxed.

"Please, Miss Castle, will you autograph something for us?" her friend corrected, shooting the other girl a frown. "We need to be respectful, Laura."

Sally closed her eyes, searching for an answer that would get her out of the situation the fastest. Luckily, the older woman had moved off to help another customer. Stepping a little off to the side, she motioned for the girls to follow. "Look, I'm so honored you want my autograph. But I'm still recovering from the accident and prefer my privacy. So if I give you an autograph, will you promise me not to tell anyone you saw me?"

"Anything, Miss Castle. This is so awesome. And we're rooting for you to come back. We all are. You're the greatest skier ever." The girl called Laura was beaming up at her, her expression one of total admiration.

"That's not true, but I'll take it." Sally grinned. It was nice to have such positive feedback after everything she had been t hrough...and was still going through. The endorsers might be pulling out, but her fans were sticking by her side. It was more than sweet. She reached into her purse and retrieved the marker and two headshot photos. They were always there, just in case, and weren't something she had bothered to remove when she came to Vermont. Which turned out to be a good thing as they would come in handy now.

"I know you're Laura," she said to one of the girls, "but what's your name?" she asked the other.

"I'm Jennifer," the young girl said, her eyes alight with excitement.

Sally autographed two photos personalizing them, and then handed one to each of the girls.

"Thank you so much. Can we get a photo with you?" Jennifer asked.

Sally glanced around, but there was no sign of Randy. "Sure." She removed her glasses again and smiled, the two girls standing next to her, one on each side. It was for a good cause, and it's not like they didn't know who she was at this point. Randy was another story entirely.

"Thank you," they both said before running off, giddy with excitement.

She turned back to the woman who had finished with the other customer, only to discover the designer watching her with renewed interest. Sally slid her glasses back on. "I'll take this," she said, picking up the pendant off the table.

"And I'm buying it for her," Randy said, appearing out of nowhere and standing beside her. He held out his credit card.

"No, you can't," Sally said, reaching out to stop him. There was no way to know what he'd seen, or not seen for that matter, his sudden presence unsettling.

"Sure I can. You did buy me a gift already, so it's only fair I return the generosity."

The designer took his card, pausing to look back and forth between the two of them. "I think he's right. Besides, a gift given in love is always to be treasured."

Sally shook her head. "It's not love—we're friends. And I gave him a potholder. They're not quite in the same league," she said, trying to defend her position.

"One must be good at giving and receiving," he teased. "Allow me." Randy held out his hand for the pendant.

"Fine," she said, placing it in the palm of his hand as the designer moved off to ring up the sale. Turning, she allowed Randy to clasp it around her neck. "What do you think?"

"Beautiful," he said, his voice huskier than a moment ago. Their eyes locked. Randy leaned forward, closing the distance between them.

She drew in a deep breath. The depth of emotion in his expression was unmistakable, and she was almost positive he wasn't referring to the necklace.

"Here you go, sir." The designer had returned, ending the moment. She handed the sales slip and credit card back to Randy. "A lovely gift for a lovely lady. See that you hang on to her. She has a beautiful spirit and deserves happiness."

"I do believe you're right about everything. I'll have to see what I can do to get Sally to agree." Randy grinned. "Merry Christmas."

"And a Merry Christmas to you both." The gleam in her eyes was enough for Sally to know she'd seen what was happening and intentionally timed the interruption.

The heart wants what the heart wants. Perhaps the woman was trying to make Sally realize what her heart desired. But it wasn't that simple. There was no room in her life for a relationship. And there wouldn't be until she retired. "Merry Christmas," she said as they moved away.

The problem was...Sally wished for a redo on the moment. It would have been a beautiful memory to keep on lockdown in her heart before she left town. Sally slid her glasses back on and rewrapped her scarf around her neck. As much as she hated to cover the lovely new pendant, the fear of being outed again prevailed.

"Thank you," she said, laying a hand on Randy's arms. "You didn't have to do this, but I love it."

It was a gift of friendship and one she would treasure forever.

Chapter Eleven

♥

WITH SO MUCH TO do, leaving the craft fair until Sally was ready was not an option. Her excitement was contagious and Randy was more than willing to go with the *shop-till-you-drop* principal. It was as if everything was a new experience, and he loved that he could share the moments with Sally. Next year, he hoped she'd be joining him for the eighth annual craft fair, something he needed to talk to her about.

With every passing hour, he was less inclined to let her walk out of his life. Even the jewelry designer understood Sally's gentle kindness was unique. The woman had gone out of her way to make sure Randy saw it as well, but she need not have worried. When he was around Sally, his life was filled with a warmth he couldn't explain. A caring about someone that went beyond friendship.

Randy pulled into the driveway at his mother's house. He turned to Sally and took her hand. "Are you sure you still want to do this?"

"Of course. Why wouldn't I? Did you forget to tell me they're terrible cooks? Or about some skeleton you have hidden in your closet you don't want me to know?" she asked, a teasing light in her eyes.

He shook his head. "Nothing like that, I promise. It's just they want me to find someone special and they are definitely on board with me leaving the military in order to make it happen. And if they started thinking about you and I in that light, there's no telling what they will say or do."

"I see. Well then, we just need to remind your family I don't live here and that we're just friends."

A friend he almost kissed. *Twice.* A friend he could swear wanted to be kissed both times. "Yes, I'm sure that will work." *Not likely.* His mother and sister wouldn't give up that easily, always looking for the happily-ever-after.

"Your mom will have dessert, won't she?" Sally asked, changing the subject.

"I'm almost positive of that. You have quite a sweet tooth, something I didn't expect. I mean, there was cocoa, and funnel cakes, peach pie, and even some fudge."

Sally shrugged. "Long story, but I haven't always eaten lots of treats. So let's just say I'm sampling culinary delights while I can." She laughed and slid out of the car, not bothering to wait for him to come around to her side.

Randy could get used to the sound of her laughter and her smile. She'd gone from nervous and looking around throughout the day to happy, smiling, and carefree. He much preferred the latter.

Ben's dream to come home and get married and start a family suddenly made sense. Sally made the pieces all fall into place as she was exactly the type of person Randy would choose to date. Except she didn't live here, and she was adamant a friendship was all she could offer. He needed to remember that and not let his heart get too caught up in the moment. But it wouldn't stop him from at least proposing the possibility of seeing her again.

His mother greeted them at the door, Misty by her side. "I'm so glad you're here, Sally. Welcome to our home." She made the introductions to his Aunt Theresa and Uncle Willy, and his sister moved forward to hug Sally like an old friend.

"Thank you for the invite. I'm traveling on business, and a home-cooked meal was more than enough temptation to say yes." Sally bent down to give Misty her own special hello hug before removing her glasses and unwinding her scarf. It was with only the slightest hesitation before she removed it, but one Randy recognized.

The house was filled with the aroma of Christmas while the Manheim Steamroller Orchestra played softly on the stereo console. Warm and welcoming. Randy had to admit, he liked what he saw. It was as though the down-home appeal was finally sinking in. He led her to the living room and held out his hand for her jacket.

"Oh, what a lovely pendant," his sister said, moving closer to inspect the opal.

"Thank you. Your brother bought it for me today," she said, her hand going to the stone.

"He did, did he? Impeccable taste, I must say. Although not something I would have given him credit for," she teased, slapping his arm playfully.

"Well, to be fair, Sally picked it out, and I simply picked up the tab. I owed her a gift since she bought me something." He grinned, shooting Sally an *I-gotcha* look.

"Oh. Interesting. And what was it that Sally got you, dear?" his mother asked.

Randy opened the bag and pulled out his gift. "A Christmas potholder. For my new home," he added, grinning.

"The home you don't even have yet. Maybe you could take it back to those fancy barracks of yours. I'm sure the guys would have a field day with teasing," Uncle Willy quipped. Everyone howled in laughter.

He might not have a house yet, but he was closer than anyone knew. The thought had stayed with him all day. The idea of leaving the military had merit, and he was reasonably sure he would do it. But a part of him was also seeing Sally in the picture. Was it possible he had found love much the way Ben had? If so, it was no wonder his friend was willing to set a new course, preferring to spend time with someone special and make a new life. Lucky for Ben, his fiancé had agreed. Not so with Sally. At least not yet.

"Let me guess, Sally picked the potholder out for you. I wonder why?" His mother asked, a devilish glint in her eyes. *But, of course, she knew why, considering Apology pie was her idea.*

Sally walked over to the Christmas tree, her hand gently touching the branches. "Is it real?" she asked, her voice almost breath-less.

Randy moved to stand next to her. Sally's face was like that of an angel as she gazed at the ornaments.

"Oh, yes. We like to support the church fundraiser, and they bring in some of the loveliest trees," his mother answered.

Sally inhaled deeply. "I love the fresh pine scent. It's like being on a walk in the woods. And the decorations are exquisite."

She moved from one to the next, touching some to turn them just right.

"Most of those are handmade. My mother kept everything my sister, and I made in school, but there's also some of her own crafts. She loves to take old photos or memorabilia and turn them into a decoration. A way of remembering the past is how she puts it," Randy said. "Here's one of my not-so-great ornaments." He chuckled, pointing at the stuffed apple that looked more like a tomato with the words *Mere Crismas* written on the side in glitter.

"Spelling expert, I see," Sally teased.

"I was five."

"Then it's perfect. It's such a beautiful tradition," Sally added.

"We have lots of those, trust me," his sister chimed in. "My husband's family didn't do much for Christmas, so it's been quite an adjustment for him. I think he loves it far more than he lets on, but don't tell him I told you so." Naomi laughed.

"The only tradition I remember was baking gingerbread cookies with my mother,"

Sally said, her tone wistful. "That was a long time ago."

"I'm sorry, dear." His mother moved to give Sally a hug.

"Thank you. She died when I was eight, but sometimes, like now, I really miss her," Sally said, wiping at her eyes with the sleeve of her shirt.

"She's in your heart, and that's something that never goes away," his mother said, her quiet wisdom comforting.

"I love gingerbread cookies," Randy said, trying to lighten the mood.

"I think you two should bake cookies together. In fact, if Sally is going to be in town during the holidays, she should share them with us. It would be so much fun to have a new face for all the excitement. What do you say, Sally? Please say you're staying in town and will join us?" His mother was turning on the charm, and Randy waited for Sally's answer.

She had already told him she would stick around and they could spend time together. But spending time with his family might not be what she had in mind.

Sally looked taken aback. *"Ummm*, I'm not sure. I may have to leave sooner than planned and then I won't be here for Christmas." She shot him an apologetic look.

It was the first Randy heard of a possible change in plans, and she'd had all day to tell him. He couldn't help the feeling of disappointment that sliced through him, but there was no way he would question her in front of the others.

"Well, drat. Randy, you need to work on her a bit more," his sister teased. "I agree with Mom—it would be fun to have Sally join us. It would be like having a sister around."

"I'll see what I can do," he said. As to convincing Sally of anything, he wasn't sure it would do any good. She did seem to dance to her own tune.

They moved to sit on the sofa, Misty laying half across Sally's feet. Not short on extroverted character, the group quickly fell into conversations with a wide range of topics...Sally fitting in like she belonged.

Naomi's husband arrived not long before dinner was served. He kissed his wife, wrapping his arms around her belly for a hug. A tug of emotion grabbed at Randy's heart. *Envy?*

"Matt, meet Sally Chastain, Randy's new friend. They met at the Crestfield Inn. Isn't it romantic?" Naomi said, smiling up at her husband.

"It's nice to meet you. Don't mind my wife; she's a hopeless romantic and wants nothing more than to find someone for her brother," Matt said, grinning.

"I told you they would do this. Don't say I didn't warn you." Randy chuckled.

"Nothing I can't handle. I'm from Colorado so take me off your list of candidates. And by the sounds of things, you haven't heard the story of how we met. It certainly wasn't at the inn." Sally shook her head and laughed, taking command of the situation.

"Story? Do tell?" Naomi asked.

Sally moved to sit down by the fire. "Not so much a story as it is a novella. He knocked me off my feet."

"So it was romantic? Where was this? I need details," Naomi said, pressing for more info.

"No. Not romantic. I mean, literally...not figuratively," Sally corrected, enjoying herself way too much at his expense.

His sister's face changed to one of shock. "Oh, good grief, Randy. Sometimes you can be such a klutz. I remember once when you tried to help carry in the groceries, and you tripped, sending the eggs flying. They landed on Mrs. Baker...our sitter. She was none too happy with you then either."

Randy felt his face grow warm. These were the stories he didn't want Sally to hear. "In my defense, my shoelace was untied. And it was your skateboard I tripped over."

"But you were the one who used it and left it out," Naomi shot back.

He shrugged. "Okay, there is that. And I guess that's why I apologized to Mrs. Baker. Although my apology to Sally was a bit more creative. I baked her a pie."

"Now we're getting somewhere. What a lovely gesture," Aunt Theresa said.

"It was mom's idea, but yeah, it worked," Randy admitted, shooting a smile at Sally.

Matt came to stand next to Sally. "You look so much like someone I know. I just can't place who."

"She gets that a lot. We were at dinner one night, and some stranger stopped to talk to her. Case of mistaken identity," Randy said.

"So it's not just me. Who did the woman think you were? Maybe it's the same person I'm thinking of," Matt said, his forehead drawn tight as he tried to force the recollection.

Sally shrugged. "I really can't remember...I was just surprised. But on the subject of eating dinner, from what I understood, we were waiting on you. And I, for one, am hungry, especially as Randy has tempted me with a dessert."

Randy couldn't help the feeling Sally had just executed a clean change of subject. Why, however, he couldn't begin to understand.

"He doesn't even know what we're having," his mother said, laughing as they all moved to the dining room.

The problem with Sally's denial in remembering the name, was how could she *not* remember? Randy couldn't help but wonder if she knew more than she was letting on, a reminder that from the very beginning, something was off. Perhaps he should have confronted her about it earlier, but now, he didn't have much choice but to let her play this out her way. But he would keep a close watch.

"Something smells delicious, Mom," Randy said, the aroma of garlic and tomatoes permeating the air as they entered the dining room.

"I thought I'd make your favorite in honor of you bringing a date to dinner," his mother said, pushing forward on her agenda.

Sally blushed three shades darker.

"I recall...you and Naomi did the asking. I simply relayed the message." His efforts to get them to back down might not work, but it was important not to let his family make her uncomfortable. He didn't want the perfect day to end on a sour note.

"Patato, Potato. She's here, and that's what counts. Sally, you can sit next to Randy. Matt, slide down to make room for our guest. We don't want her to feel isolated sitting next to strangers," his mother said, shooing his brother-in-law down to the end of the table.

"No problem. Closer to the head of the table gets me served quicker," his brother-in-law said, dropping a kiss on Naomi's head as he passed by.

Sally turned to Randy. "So, what's your favorite dinner?"

"Spaghetti with a delicious savory sauce. Made from scratch. The recipe was handed down over the generations, but I think it tastes best because it's made with love. At least, that's what my mother always told me." He shot Sally a wink.

"What a wonderful sentiment." Sally took the bowl of noodles and scooped out a generous serving.

"I like it. A man-sized portion, and she hasn't even tasted it yet. Talk about trust," Randy teased, taking the bowl of noodles from her.

"That's because I agree with you. Anything made with love is better, so it's got to be good." Her eyes glimmered in the light as she glanced his way.

The sauce was passed, the bowl filled with a mixture of fresh tomatoes, peppers, mushrooms, zucchini, onion, and yellow squash. A culinary delight of garden vegetables his mother kept on hand. Frozen fresh, he liked to call them.

"It looks wonderful," Sally said. "Thank you again for inviting me to join you all."

"It's vegetarian and yet quite hearty," his mother assured her. "When we don't know what someone eats or doesn't eat, we play it safe and leave out the meat. Oops, I almost forgot the bread." She stood and headed for the kitchen, returning moments later, and handed the basket to Matt.

"Now, this is one of my favorites," Matt said. "I like my sauce with sausage, but in its absence, give me garlic bread and I'm a happy man." He placed a few slices on his plate and passed the basket to Sally.

She, in turn, passed the basket to Randy without taking any.

"You're not having any? You don't know what you're missing," Randy said, holding the basket out to her in case she changed her mind.

Sally shook her head. "Actually, that's the problem. I do know what I'm missing. Garlic bread is addictive and not so good on the waistline."

"Neither are desserts, and you don't have a problem with those," Randy teased.

"Good point," Sally retorted, reaching for a piece of bread. "Time to live dangerously."

Naomi took the basket from Randy. "My waistline is already destroyed with kiddo here," she said, pointing to her belly. "Might as well enjoy."

"Never stopped you before you were pregnant," Matt teased.

"That's true." She grinned, taking a second piece.

"Anyone who has a problem with bread or dessert is missing out on life's finest," Uncle Willy said. "Of course, that's why I've got a belly that looks like Naomi's."

"Except at the end of nine months, yours won't disappear. You've had that belly for nigh on twenty years," Aunt Theresa teased.

"All thanks to your good cooking, woman," Uncle Willy leaned over to kiss his wife.

Everyone laughed, enjoying the fun banter.

Randy finished his dinner and stood, gathering his plate and those of anyone finished. "I'll get these rinsed," he offered.

"Thanks, dear," his mother said. "I'll help and get dessert while we're at it. Two is always better than one."

His mother followed him into the kitchen. "You know, Randy. That girl is as sweet as they come. I like her a lot, and I can tell you do too. Don't let her leave without trying to make something work, or you'll regret it."

There was no sense in denying what more than likely was obvious to everyone present tonight. "You're not telling me anything I don't know...but I'm not sure what it will take. You heard Sally—she lives in Colorado. I'm not getting a sense she's interested in a relationship."

"Nonsense, dear boy. You're smart...so figure it out." Patting his arm, she picked up the tray of desserts and carried them to the dining room, but not before he noticed the Warm Chocolate Melting Cake and French Vanilla ice cream.

Sally would love dessert, of that he was sure.

What he wasn't sure of, however, was how to convince Sally to give them a chance after she left town.

Chapter Twelve

♥

REGRET WAS BEST SERVED on an empty stomach, so for now...no regrets. Sally felt as though she was part of a family. And as for the food, she savored calorie after calorie, each dish bursting with flavor. A little extra time on the elliptical was easier to do than to say no to a home-cooked meal.

Tracy entered the dining room, a tray in her hand. Dessert. Something Sally had been looking forward to all day. His mother stopped beside Sally first, setting the tray on the edge of the table and placing one dish of chocolate cake in front of her.

It was a bit of a letdown, as plain chocolate cake wasn't exactly calorie-worthy or worth the buildup. "Thank you," Sally said, wanting to be gracious.

"It's Warm Chocolate Melting Cake," his mother explained, glancing back at the kitchen door. "Randy, hurry up with the ice cream," she hollered.

Ice cream would certainly spruce up the cake, even if it was winter and cold outside. Ice cream was a year-round winner for dessert.

"Wait till you try this," Naomi said as her mother served her. "Even the baby has learned to appreciate this treat. I know because he gets active after dessert and kicks like he's playing soccer." She laughed.

"It's the chocolate, don't let her kid you," Matt said, grinning at his wife.

Naomi held up her spoon and waved it at her husband. "It's the pudding. The baby likes pudding and ice cream *and* chocolate."

Randy came through the door, ice cream and scoop in hand. Glancing at the table, he moved to Sally's side and scooped out a large serving of French Vanilla ice cream.

Misty sauntered into the room, sitting next to Sally with a hopeful yet begging expression on her face.

"Go lay down, Misty. Dogs and chocolate don't mix," Randy ordered as he moved on to the next person.

"Thank you. But where's the pudding?" Sally asked, somewhat confused.

Matt chuckled. "It's all in there. The cake and the pudding are together. It's the richest, creamiest cake you'll ever eat. Kind of makes plain chocolate cake boring."

Which is sort of what Sally thought moments ago. Eager to try a bite now, she had to force herself to wait until everyone was served. Then, after Randy put the ice cream back in the kitchen and joined them, she picked up her spoon and followed the other's lead. Half a spoon of cake, half a spoon of ice cream. And totally delicious. *"Hmmm,"* she said, clamping a hand over her mouth as she realized she'd groaned out loud.

The others simply laughed.

"Now you know why it's a favorite. And come Christmas day, Mom serves it with peppermint sprinkles from the candy canes on the tree to make it extra special," Randy said, taking a bite. "I promise if you stick around and join us, you'll enjoy it just as much, if not more. It reminds me of the peppermint cocoa we had today."

It was tempting but out of the question. First the woman in the restaurant, then the TV airing, and to top it off, the two girls at the fair who had recognized her. It was a *three strikes* and she had to leave kind of deal. As bowl after bowl of the tasty stuff was finished off, Sally knew it was time to go. She had to get packed if she planned to head out first thing in the morning. "After we clean up, we should head back to the inn."

"What's the rush? Clean up can wait. Surely you can stay for a game of charades. We need even numbers for teams," Tracy said, making her continue to feel like a welcome guest.

"I think you've miscounted. I ruin the numbers," Sally said, doing a quick recount as she glanced around the room.

His mother shook her head. "Oh no, dear. Someone's got to judge, and that would be me."

The problem was that Sally wanted to stay. But it was only a problem if she made it one. Perhaps a bit longer wouldn't hurt, and it did have the added benefit of giving her yet another memory to take back to Colorado. "Well, okay then. If it's okay with Randy, that is." Once she was back home she wouldn't have opportunities like these, and she'd be a fool to cut the memory short.

"Okay, by me. I've always needed a good partner," he teased. "My mother isn't quite on the same level as I am when it comes to movie trivia." He gave his mother a hug and a light kiss on the cheek.

"Not my fault I don't like all the new-fangled stuff out. Give me Cary Grant or Doris Day, and I'm golden," his mother said, her eyes twinkling with delight at her son's affection.

"That you are, Mother. Golden." Randy shot Sally a wink. Linked by friendship and now as teammates...the bond between them growing with each passing minute.

They played for over an hour when suddenly Sally yawned. She glanced at her watch. There was no putting off the inevitable any longer. It was already nine, and she still had to pack. And there was the discussion with Randy she needed to have. Sally was resolved to tell Randy the truth before she left Cedar Grove knowing it was the right thing to do. And after she was gone, it wouldn't matter who knew she had been here.

"Ready to call it a night?" Randy asked. "We're ahead, so it's a good time to skedaddle."

"There is that." She grinned, coming to her feet, and stretching. "I'm sorry. I'm exhausted after walking around all day at the craft fair. Thank you all enough for such a special evening."

Randy stood, moving to get her jacket, and helped her put it on. Misty eagerly waited by the front door.

"You're so very welcome, dear. And the offer is still open for you to join us for the holidays," Tracy said, leaning in to hug Sally.

The others nodded in agreement as each one, in turn, hugged her, telling her goodbye like she was family.

It was overpowering...in a good way. "That's sweet of you to offer. I'll see what I can do, but no promises." She hated lying to them, but it was the only way without revealing her secret and why it would be necessary to leave at a moment's notice. And telling them now would ruin the evening—something she wasn't prepared to do.

Randy took her by the arm and led her to the truck, Misty following at a close distance. The dog stopped to sniff the bushes but still managed to beat them back to the truck.

"That was so much fun. Thank you for sharing your family with me," she said as he helped her into the truck.

He went around the truck, letting Misty jump in the back seat before Randy slid into the driver's seat. "Ditto on the fun sentiment. I haven't had that much fun in a long time—at least since we skied yesterday," he teased. "In all seriousness, though, you were a big hit. The family loves you, in case you couldn't tell." He started the truck and drove toward the inn.

"It was a mutual admiration society. I love how affectionate Matt is with your sister.

The way he doted on her and made sure she had everything she needed. It was a lovely thing to watch in action...two people in love. Your aunt and uncle are blessed to have each other. And your mother, I must say, is one of the sweetest people I've met."

"Thank you. I won't tell them you said all that, or it will go to their heads." He laughed, taking her hand in his and kissing the back of it as they pulled up to the inn. "Wait for me." Randy came around to her side of the truck and helped her out, drawing her close in his arms.

Her heart raced as she wondered if he would kiss her. The past two times they were interrupted, but this time it was just the two of them. And Misty, of course.

"I've been meaning to ask you something, and now seems like a good time," Randy said, his gaze never leaving her face.

So it wasn't a kiss he had in mind. Disappointment settled heavily in her stomach.

The clouds drifted in the sky, the full moon clear and shining brightly upon them. Randy lowered his head, inch by inch until at last, his mouth descended on hers.

Tender. Warm. *And definitely a kiss.*

One filled with genuine emotion, and Sally savored the connection. His arms came around her, drawing her tightly against his chest. Time stood still as he kissed her. And right there and then, Sally knew she didn't want to leave. *Wouldn't* leave until she had no other choice. She wasn't going to run away out of fear of discovery. Life was to be lived to the fullest, and right now, that included Randy.

He stepped back, his expression one of caring...and something else. Sally didn't dare to hope for more. Randy didn't know everything about her, but what he did know if she wasn't mistaken...he liked. Which is precisely why she couldn't tell him the truth. Just for once, she wanted to have something real with someone who liked her for herself.

"You sort of indicated you might have to leave sooner than you promised. I was hoping to change your mind and convince you to stay longer. And if your leg is better, perhaps we could hit the slopes again tomorrow. Like another date," he asked, a gleam in his eyes.

Sally let out a deep breath, relieved they were thinking alike. "You are very convincing person. And yes, I'll stay as promised. And yes, we have a ski date tomorrow." Skiing for fun with a handsome man was in a class all by itself when it came to adventure.

Randy's answering smile made the decision totally worth it. "Awesome." He let the dog out of the truck and they headed inside the inn. Always the perfect gentleman, he walked Sally to her door. "We can meet for breakfast at eight in the Bistro. Goodnight, sweet Sally," he said, his voice dropping a notch as he brushed her cheek with his thumb.

"Goodnight," she said, watching him walk down the hall before she went into her own room.

Chapter Thirteen

F OR FIVE DAYS, THE two of them had been inseparable. Skiing, dining, caroling, and spending time with his family. They even made angels in the snow, something he would have thought was just for kids. At least, he had thought that until he shared the experience with a woman who seemed to be the center of his newfound peace and joy.

And then there were the kisses. Gentle, sweet kisses that conveyed emotions previously unknown to him. Sally was different, and Randy was almost positive he knew why.

He was falling in love with her.

And come Christmas, he didn't want it to end. At some point, he would need to bring up the subject of seeing Sally beyond her visit to Cedar Grove. And up until now, he had been willing to let things continue to develop at a natural pace. It was as though she had become a part of his life, almost as naturally as he breathed. His friend Ben had totally understood how the right woman could make life sweeter. Worth moving in a new direction. Was it possible Sally was the right woman that he could love and cherish, till death do they part?

He gazed at her across the room, seeing Sally in a new light.

Tonight was the night. The official asking her to be his girlfriend and enter into a dating relationship. But that could only happen if he could find a way to put an end to the never-ending family-fun poker game everyone had been playing since dinner. Otherwise, they would sleep half the day away.

Only three players remained in the game—Sally, Naomi, and Matt. And it was Sally who appeared to be in the driver's seat at the moment, her chip stack twice that of Matts. Naomi, on the other hand, was struggling to stay in the game. Cool as can be, Sally's only show of emotion was after a winning hand was played...which seemed to happen often.

"I know you don't want to hear this, but we need to leave soon, Sally," Randy said, laying a hand on her shoulder as he came to stand behind her at the table.

"Just give me a couple more minutes. These two are going down. Finally." Sally grinned. "And I've got the hand to do it," she boasted.

He glanced down at her cards. Three queens and a king kicker. Another winning hand, for sure. "If you say so." Randy wasn't about to give any hints one way or the other, but he would let her play this out.

"I think she's bluffing," Naomi said, tapping her remaining chip stack. "I've got nothing to lose. All in." She pushed the stack to the center of the table.

Matt nodded. "I've got a lot more at stake here, but I think my wife is right. Sally has got a gleam in her eye that says she's trying to pull a fast one." He started to push both his remaining stacks toward the center but stopped. "Unless the bluffer isn't bluffing. Maybe she's trying to use reverse psychology."

Sally looked up at Randy and winked, laid her cards down on the table, and waited. Almost like a black widow waiting on her prey.

"There's no way she can have another good hand. So all in," Matt declared, shoving his chips to the center.

"Call." The one word said it all as Sally flipped over her cards. "You're right. It's not a good hand—it's an excellent one," she teased, reaching to pull the chips her way.

"Looks like you all have a winner, and it's about time. Mom and the rest of us have been out of the running for over an hour," Randy said. "We'll let the losers put away the chips."

"Good win," Matt said. "Not my night, I reckon."

"Or mine," Naomi frowned as she picked up the chips. "At least we aren't playing for money. That wouldn't have been pretty. This way, it'll give me another chance to beat you."

"You're on." Sally grinned, coming to her feet.

Randy went to get her jacket and helped her into it. "Mom, can you keep Misty tonight? We're going to hit the slopes early, and it will be easier if I don't have to stop here to drop her off."

His mother nodded while at the same time emitting a yawn. "Sure. She can keep me company."

"Thank you. Good night, everyone." Randy leaned down to kiss his mother on the cheek.

"Good night. Thank you all for another lovely evening," Sally said.

After farewells were exchanged, Randy led her out to his truck. They drove back to the inn, nervous anticipation settling in the pit of his stomach like grasshoppers on caffeine.

He parked, and then coming around the vehicle, helped her out. The moonlight cast a glow over the snow and was nothing short of romantic.

And the perfect place to pop the question. Randy stopped and pulled her into his arms, brushing her lips with a gentle kiss. "There's something I'd like to ask you."

Sally drew back. She couldn't let him take the next step between them without him knowing the truth. "I need to tell you something too," Sally said in a rush before chickening out. The past five days had been heavenly, but she sensed they might very well end by the time she finished explaining. They had become close, and the connection between them was strong. *But was it enough?*

"You go first," he said, brushing her hair off her face. "I think you know what I'm going to ask," he teased.

"The thing is—"

"It's her," someone shouted from the front porch of the inn. Suddenly a rush of people surged in their direction, spotlights, and cameras rolling.

Sally stepped back. "I'm sorry," she mumbled. Her time had run out and keeping Randy out of the limelight was a priority. "You should head inside," she urged, giving him a nudge to get moving.

Randy looked about to argue. "What's—

"Please," she said, "it's for your own good. Trust me. I'll explain later."

Randy glanced at the reporters and then back at her. He shook his head—message received. Then, turning, he walked away.

Flashes of light popped off, one after another as reporters snapped pictures. "Miss Castle, why are you here? Have you been here the whole time? Why are you in hiding?" A barrage of questions were fired at her as the media clamored for information.

She held up her hand. "I'm not prepared to answer any questions at this time. I'll arrange a full press conference when I return to Vail." Sally had learned the art of controlling her emotions and reactions to their presence. It came with the territory of being in the public eye. But it didn't mean everything had to be on their terms.

"Who's the man? Is he why you're here secretly? And what of Bobby? Is the fact he's dating someone, why you're hiding out? Or did you break up because of this new guy? What's his name?" The questions continued to come, and no one allowed her to pass through the group. The last thing she wanted to do was supply fodder for the tabloids.

"Excuse me, everyone. Sally has already said no questions. So if you don't want to be excluded from the press meeting when it's called, I suggest you do as she asks," a man's raised voice spoke from the back of the group.

Daddy? Her father was here. And at that moment, Sally didn't mind. He'd always handled the reporters for her, and he'd see to them now as well.

Amidst much grumbling, the crowd dispersed. Her father came to stand beside her, leaning in for a hug. "We'll talk inside where we are certain to have privacy."

They made their way to the front steps, with not so much as one word between them. Her father held the door open for her to enter first.

"You've led me on a merry chase, young lady, and I don't even know why. I've been worried about you. Please tell me you're done with whatever it is you've been doing, and you're ready to come back to Vail?" he said as soon as the front door closed.

Business as always. *Just once, it would be nice to have her father be...fatherly.* "I'm sorry. I needed to get away. It's hard to explain, but the accident, and my leg, and the surgeries. It was all too much."

"We have the best physical therapists and doctors at our disposal. If there's any chance of you skiing again, you need to come home."

Everything started to spin. It was the same cycle Sally tried to break free from, but nothing had changed. "Do you hear yourself? Can't this ever be about me? Your daughter. Not Sally Castle...professional skier." Her eyes filled with tears, blurring her vision.

"But this is your life we're talking about. Your future. A future you and I have built together, and one about to disappear," her father said, stating the obvious but failing to understand her point entirely.

She loosened her scarf, the warmth of the room stifling. "You don't get it. I'm tired. I don't even know if I want to ski anymore." Sally sucked in a few deep breaths of air.

Her father shook his head and frowned. "Don't say that. It's called fear. Everyone goes through it after a terrible accident. It just takes time, and we need to get you back on the slopes. Trust me on this."

Sally crossed her arms over her chest and closed her eyes for a few seconds, trying to regroup. Then, opening them, she squared off with her father. "I've already been on the slopes."

His mouth dropped open. "You skied? That's fantastic news. How did it go?" he asked in a rush of excitement.

"It was okay, given the circumstances. But nothing noteworthy, and certainly no indication of how things will turn out. Speed is sub-par at best." Not to mention, the mental aspect of committing oneself to plunge down a mountain at breakneck speeds was non-existent at this point.

"Excellent news. So are you ready to come home? We've got a lot of work to do."

Sally let out a deep sigh. She had known this could happen at some point, but she had thought there would be more time. "Yes. I'm ready." It was the only answer she could give, knowing all her father had done for her over the years.

"Addison? Is everything okay?" an older woman asked as she joined them. "I was just getting ready to go outside and find you." Neatly dressed in a white pea coat, matching hat, and boots, she was the picture of elegance.

"Yes, Marion. I'd like you to meet my daughter, Sally Castle. She's returning to Vail with me," he announced, the pride in his voice unmistakable.

The woman smiled and held out her hand. "It's nice to meet you. Your father talked non-stop all day, and he's quite proud of you."

Sally shook hands. "It's nice to meet you also. What do you mean all day?"

Her father nodded. "Yes, I've been here since around eight, but you'd already left. The guy at the front desk wouldn't tell me where you went, so I waited around."

Kyle, it appeared, used discretion at his own whim. Sally would need to remember to thank him. "I was with a friend all day."

"And evening, considering it's after nine," he added.

Sally didn't want to talk about the day with Randy or the family night she had spent with the Grangers, so she remained silent.

Marion laid her hand on her father's arm. "It wasn't all bad, don't let him fool you. After our breakfast orders got switched up somehow, and we realized what happened, we opted to eat breakfast together. There was no sense in letting the food go to waste. Your father is an interesting man and quite dedicated to your success. What a blessing that must be for you."

A mixed blessing at this point. "It has been. I couldn't have accomplished any of my success without my father by my side," Sally said, stating the truth. Even if the truth was shifting, it didn't change the past.

"Marion's right. It did make for an interesting day as she took pity on me, and we went for a walk, had lunch and dinner, and even squeezed in a few games of backgammon while we waited. I mean while *I* waited. You know what I mean," he said, suddenly sounding unsure of himself.

"You played games?" Sally asked, dumbfounded. This was a side of her father that hadn't existed since her mother passed away.

Her father nodded, somewhat embarrassed. "Yes, we played games. Just because I haven't had time in years doesn't mean I've forgotten how," he teased.

"I see." Sally couldn't help but wonder if the fun factor in her father was solely due to Marion and that he was actually crushing on the woman. She gazed at Marion with renewed interest.

"So, who was the guy you were with today?" her father asked, changing the subject back to a topic she preferred to skip.

"No one special. He's just a friend I met on the slopes and skied with," she said, trying to sound nonchalant. A movement on the stairs caught her attention.

Randy. He stood frozen at the bottom of the staircase, duffle bag in hand. By the looks of things he intended to leave without so much as a word to her.

She hadn't meant the comment the way it sounded, and it was obvious Randy had heard. The words were more an effort to throw her father off what was closer to the truth—that she cared far more about Randy than she should.

Sally was sure it wouldn't bode well if her father interrogated Randy, knowing it could sully anything developing between them. Besides, she had managed to do enough of that on her own. And her father's spiel was like a recording—one Sally heard far more often than she liked.

"Oh, no. This doesn't look good at all. Talk about tension," Captain Tremont said with a shake of his head.

"Shhh," Chloe hushed him, putting a finger to her lips.

"That can't hear us, my dear."

"There's more going on between Sally and her father than we know," Chloe said in a low voice, ignoring his comment.

"I can't help but agree, my dear. And it's a shame your efforts to keep Mr. Castle from leaving straightaway failed. However, I do believe,

given a couple of days, he and Marion might have made a connection."

"Oh, they made a connection all right. It's getting that man to act on what was right in front of this face. Did you see the way he looked at her? The more time those two spent together, the more relaxed he got. Not at all like the uptight curmudgeon who arrived early this morning in search of Sally. He needs to focus on someone other than his daughter. She's a grown woman, for goodness sake."

Captain Tremont nodded. "Mixing up the breakfast orders was good thinking. I'm not sure how you knew it would work, but it did."

"I didn't know. But after I heard Addison Castle on the phone, I had to do something to keep him from leaving and turning the town upside down looking for Sally. I wanted nothing to get in the way of those two having more time together—not even her father. Which it did anyway, in the end. I just wish I knew what to do to fix things. Sally's leaving in the morning with her father, and then what? Do we accept that we failed to get them to see what's right in front of them? I just know in my heart those two are right for each other. And for that matter, so are Sally's

father and Marion. Why can't people open their hearts and see beyond the surface?" Chloe crossed her arms in front of her chest and let out a deep, wistful sigh.

"The same reason I didn't see past the obvious when I first met you, my dear. It took two hundred years for me to figure it out," Captain Tremont said, smiling down at Chloe with love in his eyes.

"Yes, but that's because Claire always stole the limelight. It's an older twin thing." Chloe smiled, remembering her sister's antics.

"She did like to be the life of the party. But then, maybe that's why these people need you and your insight. You help them find true love, so they don't miss out."

"We help them find true love, not just me," Chloe said, bestowing the captain with a loving gaze. It was easy to wear her heart on her sleeve when this man was around. "We need to pay attention. By the looks of things, we may not be able to salvage this romance and it simply breaks my heart."

"It's not over yet, my dear. Not with you around." The captain took her in his arms and

kissed her before stepping back, still holding one hand.

Chloe leaned forward, intent on hearing what the others were saying in the hopes a miracle would present itself.

Chapter Fourteen

♥

"*No one special. Just a friend I met on the slopes and skied with.*" Randy's stomach clenched, Sally's words echoing in his head. It was more than enough to solidify his decision to leave the inn and more than enough to know the truth of how Sally felt about him. A one-sided relationship would never end happily. Hoping to make an exit without being spotted, he made a beeline for the door.

"Randy, wait. We need to talk," Sally called out.

So much for leaving unnoticed. He turned back. "I think everything that needs saying has been said. Or can be read between the lines. Or maybe even on the front page of the paper in the morning." The sarcasm in his voice was unavoidable given the situation.

"It's not what you think. I mean, it is, but I can explain," Sally said, catching up to him and reaching for his arm.

"Careful, Sally. Daddy's watching. You wouldn't want him to get the wrong idea about our friendship." He delivered the dig, making sure she knew he had heard the comment.

Sally stepped back, glancing at her father and then at him, her expression unreadable. "I'm sorry. You're right. I should go."

Her words were his cue to leave. Randy dropped the key at the front desk and headed for the door, only to have his way blocked. Mr. Castle, aka daddy, obviously had a thing or two to say.

"Addison Castle." Sally's father held out his hand, his steely gaze sizing Randy up from head to toe.

"Randy Granger." Good manners had him shaking hands with the guy. Besides, his beef was with his daughter, not her daddy.

"I hear you've been spending time with my daughter. Anyone she spends time with normally has to go through me first, but she was on a short hiatus from her regular way of life. She's returning to Colorado with me in the morning. Her time and dedication to a full recovery will be valuable, and her emotional well-being even more so."

Randy glanced over at Sally as she stood deep in conversation with a woman by the fireplace, her back ramrod stiff. "And your point?" Randy asked. It was past time for him and Misty to leave.

"My point is, don't start seeing wedding bells with my daughter. Few men wouldn't want a woman as beautiful as she is, not to mention, as famous." His warning was clear and more than a little insulting.

And it was also where good manners went out the door. "You have nothing to worry about, sir. I didn't even know your daughter was Sally Castle until moments ago. Had I known, you and I wouldn't be having this conversation." Although truth be told, he didn't know if that part was true. But then, they would never know, seeing as she hadn't bothered to tell him the truth.

Addison's steely gaze intensified, his pursed lips radiating the man's tension. "Care to explain? That is my daughter you're talking about."

Randy shrugged, not in the least intimidated by the man. It was a life he never understood and didn't need to. "There's nothing to explain. I like Sally Chastain. A lot. I don't know Sally Castle, other than what I've seen on the television. That's popularity I could do without." The closest he came to popularity was student body president in high school, which was more than enough to sour him on the prospect. The stumping for votes. Everyone watching you all of the time, waiting for you to make a mistake. People think you held all the answers to every problem. *No, thank you.*

Addison's frown deepened if it were possible. He glanced back at Sally. "I see. Very interesting."

Randy shook his head. "Not really. Now, if you'll excuse me, I'm going home." Once outside, he took a deep breath of cold air, trying to calm the rush of disappointment and heartache with the turn of events. He slid into the driver's side and drove home, Addison's warning repeating itself in his head. It's not like Sally was sixteen and still in high school, but her father still treated her as if she were.

He still couldn't believe everything that had just happened in the space of fifteen minutes or less. The kiss. The reporters. Sally's dismissal. He'd hung back at the edge of the crowd for a few minutes, enough to figure out what was going on. He also knew Sally had made a fool of him. All this time, he thought he was trying to protect her from something or someone, and all she was doing was hiding out from the media. *And her father.*

Sally Castle. Professional skier. Olympic and World Cup winner. Athlete extraordinaire. But definitely *not* Sally Chastain.

Randy had stood off to the side to keep an eye on things from a distance, his need to protect Sally strong. But after she'd acknowledged the man who approached was her father, he had gone inside the inn. She didn't need him for protection...or anything else for that matter.

Thinking back over the past week and a half, he shook his head. "Ski lessons. What an idiot," he said, slapping himself on the side of his head. "Good grief." Sally must have been having a huge laugh at his expense.

What a fool he'd been—in many ways. No wonder people scoffed at the premise of *love at first sight*. He'd given his heart to a fraud. A woman who couldn't even be honest with him. Was he that desperate for the American dream of a home and family? The wrong woman could be just as devastating as no woman.

Except he couldn't get the kiss out of his head. It had been practically perfect in every way. But apparently, it hadn't meant anything to her. But then why would it, seeing as he was just a country boy from Cedar Grove and she was the world-famous Sally Castle. They never stood a chance because none of it had been real.

Sally was welcome to her world, but it wasn't one Randy wanted any part of. He believed in truth because, without it, there could be no trust. And without trust, there could be no love.

Love. A silly illusion he'd fallen into on the mountain slopes of Bolton Valley.

But like all illusions, they ended. And it was precisely why he was going home to a packed house and a sofa, something that sounded a whole lot more appealing than staying another minute at the Crestfield Inn with Sally and her father.

Randy couldn't help recalling bits and pieces of their conversations. *She was on business. In the sports industry. Worked with her father and traveled.* It was all there. She hadn't exactly lied, but then, her answers were vague enough to give information without details. Sally had been very good at evasion.

He pulled into the driveway, not looking forward to an inquisition from his family. Using his key to unlock the door, he entered, dropping his duffle bag in the foyer. "Hello," he called out when he heard voices, not wanting to alarm anyone. "It's just me." Misty came running, dancing excitedly when she spotted him. "Hey, girl," he said, patting her side.

His mother flipped on the light. "Keep your voice down. Your aunt and uncle have already gone to bed. So what are you doing back here? Did you forget something? And where's Sally?" she asked, tossing out the questions like he was coming in late on a school night. Until her gaze landed on his bag. "Did you two have a fight?"

Randy let out a deep breath. "You could say that."

"Come in, come in," his mother said, taking him by the arm and leading him to the living room.

"What's going on? And where's Sally?" Naomi asked. Snuggled up on the couch with Matt, the two presented a picture of peaceful wedded bliss. Something Randy wanted, but apparently, it wasn't meant to be. At least not yet. He'd picked the wrong woman, something he would have to rectify. *Someday. Just not yet.*

"They had a fight," his mother offered.

"Tell us what you did?" his sister said, shaking her head.

Randy glared at her, but he tempered his response. "Seriously? Me? Thanks for the vote of confidence." He sat in the rocker, and Misty lay down next to him.

"Well, everything was going so great when you left," his mother said, not taking the hint. "We all talked about what a lovely person she is and hoped you two would see what we saw—a couple in love."

"*Hmmmph.* What you saw was a lie. What you saw was someone who didn't exist. So none of it was real," Randy ground out.

"Have you had too much to drink? You're not making any sense," Naomi interjected.

"I don't drink, and you know it."

"Let the guy talk, you two. Around the Granger women, it can be hard to get a word in edgewise," Matt said, taking his wife's hand and kissing it to soften the words.

A smooth move for sure, and Randy appreciated his brother-in-law's help. "Let me be clear, so I don't have to repeat this again, seeing as I really don't want to talk about it in the first place. The woman here tonight was none other than Sally Castle...the missing skier the media made a big deal of finding. Sally Chastain doesn't exist."

All three people in the room fell silent.

"You've got to be kidding? Sally Castle was here and had dinner with us? That is totally cool," Matt said, recovering from the shock.

Randy wasn't inclined to agree with his brother-in-law's point of view. "I'm glad someone thinks so. Our friendship was a lie. And to think I gave her ski lessons. What an idiot," he said, running a hand through his hair and propping his feet up on the coffee table as he sat back.

His mother moved closer. "Ski lessons, huh? It can't be as bad as all that. She just didn't want to hurt your feelings. And no feet on the table, this is not a horse's stable," his mother said, smacking at his feet until he lowered them to the floor.

"How can you defend her? She lied."

Naomi shook her head. "Technically, she omitted the truth and for an excellent reason. If she wanted to avoid a media circus and find somewhere to recover from the accident, then she went about it all the right way." Leave it to his sister to defend Sally even knowing the truth.

But then, anything that got in the way of the Granger women agenda was insignificant. And their agenda was him and Sally as a couple. "You mean the wrong way, don't you? Lying?"

"I agree with Naomi. You keep quiet if you're trying to avoid the media and don't know who to trust. She did what she needed to do to protect herself. Other than that, the woman you spent time with is still the same Sally. I'm sure she would have told you eventually," his mother said, defending his sister's opinion.

Told you eventually. The words reminded him that Sally had been about to tell him something. *After the kiss*. Had it been the kiss and tell moment? "Maybe. Maybe not. Guess we'll never know."

"So, just like that, you give up on her?" Naomi asked, glaring at him.

Randy shrugged. "It's not like I have a choice in the matter. Her father is here to take her home. She doesn't need me, and he confirmed she's leaving in the morning. Can we change the subject, please?"

"Fine, for tonight. But we're not done talking about this. I saw the way you looked at each other, and it was love in your eyes. You two need to figure out what's important in life and go for it," his mother said, moving closer to the fire.

"Sally made her choice. Skiing is her life, and she's all in. There's no room for a relationship. And her father made sure I understood the rules. Now, since I need to sleep on the couch, is there any way you all can retire to the kitchen so I can go to bed? It's been a long day," Randy said, standing to emphasize his point.

Murmurs of agreement sounded around the room, and one by one, they filed out.

His mother stopped to kiss him on the cheek. "I'm truly sorry, darling. But don't give up on Sally just yet. Promise me that much."

"Sure thing, Mom." It wouldn't do any good to argue with her, but the truth was, he had given up. The wall around his heart was all that he had left to protect himself from heartbreak. *If it hadn't already.*

He wanted a future with someone he could trust, someone who valued stability in life. And for Sally Castle...her life was anything but stable. Instead, her life was a never-ending cycle that would take her around the world for however long her career lasted.

A life that had no room for distractions.

And he would be a distraction...her father had been clear on the subject.

Chapter Fifteen

♥

"I've got to hand it to you, Sally, but whatever you were doing in Cedar Grove seems like it worked well. Your strength is almost back to one hundred percent. But, unfortunately, we have no way to know about control and mechanics until you hit some runs and try to do what I once thought would never happen. Your return to professional skiing," the doctor said, shaking his head as if he still couldn't believe it.

"My father will be thrilled to hear you say it," Sally said, unsure how she felt about the news. It's what she'd been pushing for the past week, or at least she thought that was the goal. And as to what she had been doing? That was easy to answer...she'd been taking time off from the professional aspects of skiing and all the craziness associated with it. It had been a time to step back and return to the basics. A way to regain her confidence without the pressure to perform.

And now that the doctor was confirming what Sally had already thought possible, the next step was to do timed runs. The World Pro Ski Women's downhill competition was only three days away. It was almost crazy to even think of entering, but that's precisely what she was considering. It had always been a dream to win at Beaver Creek—the place where she trained and her hometown.

So why elation wasn't her first response, she couldn't begin to imagine. Maybe in her heart, skiing no longer brought her the same joy she once felt. Or maybe, truth be told, she was afraid. The crash had left an impact, and it was only normal to experience the trepidation to commit heart and soul and push-off, catapulting down the mountain. And with her sights on the fall line and knowing that one mistake could be costly.

She was fortunate to be able to return...some skiers never got over the fear or the injuries. It was like a blessing and a curse at the same time. The ability and the drive all present but laced with a heavy dollop of fear.

"I agree with you there," the doctor said, shaking his head. "Your father is determined to prove everyone wrong and to say he was right, of course. However, he needs to give you credit for the return as your time in Cedar Grove seems to have been the right therapy."

If the doc only knew the truth. It was more about Randy than skiing. Or a little bit of both. Or a lot of Randy and a little bit of skiing. The last choice came closer to the truth. "Thanks, and I know you're right, but Dad has always been this way. I'm guessing he's not going to change."

"Probably not, but then unless I'm way off the mark here, I get the sense you have." The doctor was busy scribbling something on a file, but his comment was insightful, and one Sally wasn't sure how to respond to.

"Maybe. But let's keep that between you and me. Right now, I've got timed trials to get past if I want to race Saturday at Beaver Creek."

"Just think this through, Sally. I feel like you're pushing too hard, and this is too soon. Ease back into this." The doctor pushed his glasses up a notch on his nose, his eyes filled with concern. It would be a tough place to keep a patient safe and yet, not stifling their need to compete, something athletes train for all their lives.

"This race won't come back to Vail for years and definitely not within my racing career. It's one I've always wanted to win. And I may not be able to win it given the circumstances, but I want to compete. I deserve a shot, and I won't walk away." Before the accident, it was all she talked about. It was difficult to even imagine not giving it a shot, if only for her own sense of pride and accomplishment. Not admitting defeat. It was her can-do attitude that had gotten her this far, and she would continue to tap the same well. It wasn't a dry well...not by a long shot.

"Okay then if you're sure. I'll sign the waiver. Just please, be careful. I'm telling you this as your doctor, but also as your friend. I've watched you grow up and become a beautiful young woman, both inside and out, and would hate it if anything goes wrong because I gave in to your ambitions."

"Gotcha, doc." She shot him a smile of gratitude and hopped off the table. "I'll be ultra-careful and come in last place," she teased. "Thank you for the vote of confidence, as I most certainly need it." Sally headed out the door, eager to be away from the docs prying eyes.

If he could read her mind, he'd know all the doubts that existed there. This was something Sally had to do for herself. And once the sponsors got wind she had been cleared to ski, there was no telling how quickly they would line up again to offer new contracts. Something desperately needed if she didn't want to bankrupt her father. Skiing was mighty expensive and not for the weak in spirit or finances.

After she arrived home, Sally pulled out her phone, intent on calling Jessica. After delaying her departure, her friend had only just come from Canada because of the handsome man she'd met at the Lake Louisa races. He was also more than likely the reason her friend hadn't done well in the race.

She pressed the keypad icon, her finger accidentally catching the one next to it. Her photo album opened, and a familiar picture popped up on the screen. It was the day of the craft fair, a most memorable day for Sally.

Silliness had won over by late afternoon, and she'd taken a selfie of the two of them standing behind Santa and telling the jolly old man what they wanted for Christmas. Sally touched Randy's face on the screen. Lit with excitement, his grin had crinkled the corners of his eyes. It was only when she was alone that she allowed herself the luxury to remember their moments together. The memories of fun and laughter etched in her mind.

And then there was their last day together. One that hadn't ended well. She should have told Randy long before any feelings had been acknowledged between them. And the kisses. He had every right to be angry with her and there was nothing she could say that would have changed anything. Which is why she had admitted defeat and walked away.

A move she regretted. Sally should have made Randy listen...but now it was too late.

What they had shared was genuine, and it was what made their friendship different. More personal. She closed the app, unwilling to let herself get sidetracked. Her phone rang just as she was about to slide it into her purse. "Hey, Dad. I'm guessing you heard?"

"I'm not sure what you're talking about. I called because you need to turn on Channel 11. They're talking about you," he said.

The media talking about Sally Castle was nothing new. They had gone on and on about her accident and the injuries, replaying the whole nightmare in case anyone hadn't seen it. The conjecture about her prospects of returning to professional skiing was old news, but she flipped on the TV anyway.

Sally watched as the reporter spoke with two young girls, their faces familiar. It instantly dawned on her it was Jennifer and Laura from the craft fair. *So much for them not talking to the press.*

"What was she like when you met her?" the reporter asked, flipping her long brown hair off her face and smiling into the camera before turning it back to the girls.

"Sally, I mean, Miss Castle was fabulous. It was so cool," Jennifer said, grinning from ear to ear.

"It was a dream come true. Miss Castle was so nice to us. She gave us autographs and took a selfie with her. How cool is that?" Laura chimed in.

"Do you know what Sally Castle was doing in Cedar Grove?" the reporter asked.

"Nope. She just asked us not to tell anyone that we saw her. And we kept our promise. Pinky swear, if you're listening to this Miss Castle." The girls locked their pinkies for all to see. "But we figure after it was on the news, we could tell our friends we met her. It's not like it was a secret anymore."

"I want to be just like her when I grow up," Laura said, the admiration in her voice undeniable.

"Me too," Jennifer exclaimed, not to be outdone.

So if it wasn't the two girls, chances are it was the woman in the restaurant who had outed her location. Or it could have been anyone else who recognized her, especially given that with Randy, she had relaxed her guard. In the end, it didn't matter who, only that it had been done. And that it cut short her time with Randy.

The excitement of the two girls was infectious, and it was something Sally had lost sight of. They hadn't wanted autographs because she *couldn't* ski. Instead, they admired her when she *could* and aspired to be like her. Now wasn't the time to cower away behind her injuries. Sally needed to suck it up and show her fans the grit and determination to come back from adversity. Show them what it took to be a world-class professional athlete.

She would do this. "I'm going to do it, Dad. The World Pro Ski women's downhill competition right here in Beaver Creek."

"But you need clearance from the doctor, and that's only days away. I'm thrilled you are mentally ready to return. I'm just not sure we can make it happen this fast. Or that it's advisable yet."

"I got clearance today. Timed trials are tomorrow," Sally said, a hint of satisfaction in her voice. There were no guarantees of tomorrow on the circuit, her accident a startling reminder of the truth. But the last thing she wanted to do was end her career on a sour note. It was all people would remember. More importantly, it was all she would remember.

"That's awesome, honey. Are you sure? Too soon could be dangerous," he said, his hesitation more than a little concerning.

This wasn't the Addison Castle she knew and loved. "What? I thought you wanted this. Why are you questioning my decision?"

"I want what's best for you. That's all I've ever wanted, sweetheart."

"This is for the best. I promise," Sally said, trying to sound more confident than the knots in her stomach laid claim to.

"Then let's do this. I'm right behind you. Always have been and always will be."

Sally hung up the phone and grabbed her jacket. She needed to get some runs in for practice before the timed trials.

Anything worth doing was worth doing well.

Randy sensed someone had come into the room and he opened his eyes, only to discover his mother standing over him. Misty returned to sleep mode, ignoring his mother's presence. Randy wished he could do the same but also knew he wouldn't be so lucky. "What's up, Mom?" he asked, determined to get whatever the conversation was about over. Then he could go back to napping.

"It's been days since she left, and you're still walking around in your own little world playing what-if games. I know you all too well, so don't try to pull the wool over my eyes," his mother scolded.

They both knew she meant Sally. The whole house hadn't stopped talking about the professional skier who had come to dinner. And then, just as quickly, left town. There were many interviews on TV, and Sally's smiling face showed that she was back in her element. "Everything will be fine. I'm just trying to make some decisions about the Army. You know that, too. It's a big decision and not one to be made lightly. And there's Misty to consider."

The dog lifted her head and laid her chin on Randy's leg. He reached out and patted her side.

"And I get that. But if you care about Sally the way I believe you do, you're doing the both of you a disservice by not discussing it. You need to fight for what you love, son."

Love. It wasn't a word he had applied to his feelings, but it would certainly explain the heartache he had felt since she had left. He had fought for his country out of love. So why wouldn't he fight for a woman he thought he loved? *Okay, so most likely loved, the words sounding genuine in his head.* "I'll think about it, Mom."

"Well, if you'd turn on the TV and keep up, you'd find out Sally is skiing again. They just announced it today."

"She is?" he asked, suddenly sitting up and interested.

"Yes. Sally is going to compete in the pro women's downhill race right before Christmas in Vail. She posted good times on her trials, and although there's huge speculation whether she's ready or not, you've got to hand it to her for trying. Takes guts if you ask me." His mother was clearly still a huge fan of Sally, no matter what else had happened. She leveled him with a glare—her message loud and clear.

"I said I would think about it. And for the record, it's not about having the guts to go see Sally. She lied. Let's not forget that, please. It's hard to start a relationship on a lie." He had gone over this repeatedly, and nothing had changed. And if he returned to the base and stayed in the military, it was a moot point. They would both be traveling, and it's not like they could sustain a relationship.

"She had good cause, and you know it. I doubt life has been easy for her to get where she's at. You've been thinking about getting out of the military, so why not do it? For yourself. And as an oh, by the way, it would give you a chance to see what you could work out with Sally."

"Maybe," he said, unwilling to commit one way or the other. His mother meant well, but this was something he needed to work out on his own.

"Are you afraid of risking everything and ending up with nothing?" his mother asked, not giving up on their discussion.

She always had been a persistent woman and likely where he got it from. "Maybe."

"Life is about taking risks. Happiness comes to those who seek it, not those sitting back and waiting silently for it to happen. Think on it." His mother turned and walked away.

Randy grabbed the remote and flipped on the sports channel. It wasn't long before a picture of Sally flashed across the screen. So bright, smiling, and beautiful. The woman he loved. He tested the notion in his head, and it sounded more than a little right.

The sportscaster recapped most of what his mother had already mentioned. Sally would race again. He knew this would be an important moment in her life, and he would be an idiot not to share it with her. It would be the perfect opportunity to talk with her and see how she felt about him. And his mother was right—if he left the Army, there was nothing to stop him from traveling with her.

After all, home is where the heart is, and if his feelings were this strong after weeks, he couldn't begin to imagine what it would be like after more time with her.

Decision made, Randy was left to put his plan into action. He would fly to Denver and drive to Vail to Sally. The stability he craved would be in his love for her, not a home in one town.

If Sally loved him back.

And there was only one way to find out.

Chapter Sixteen

♥

SALLY PULLED INTO THE parking lot and glanced up at the slopes. Vail hosted some of the finest world-class skiing trails, and it still amazed her to think she had been lucky enough to grow up here. It was also where she started her formal training to prepare her for the racing world.

The snow was powder soft. Sally used to think it made for an easier landing when she fell, rather than the hard ice sometimes found in other more humid climates. But she soon discovered the faster you went, the falls hurt anyway.

She'd give anything to go back home and crawl under the covers. Race day. One race. Top to bottom. *And she was terrified.*

The timed trials had been about qualifying and her point rankings. The downhill race was about speed. A hundredth of a second could mean the difference between winning and simply finishing. This was about finding the fall line and sticking to it without fear. And not something Sally was sure she could do today. It was too soon. Or too late. Or too anything.

"Let's get a move on, Sally," her father called out, slinging her gear pack over his shoulder, his other arm firmly around Marion. The two had become an item, something that still surprised Sally.

And made her heart ache for Randy.

Her father had always believed in Sally, and it had always been just the two of them. The pressure to win and make him proud and to repay him for all the hours and money he had spent helping her achieve her dream was enormous. She was happy he had finally taken an interest in something else. Or someone else in this case. But she also wondered how it would all play out. Racing took up so many hours in a day, and there wasn't much time left for building relationships. Something Sally knew all too well.

Within minutes of her arrival the media reporters spotted her. They began clamoring for an interview, asking a question, or just talking about the race and capturing photos or footage of her. Anything to appeal to the viewers. Why they would want to watch her stretch or gear up, she didn't have a clue. But there was no such thing as privacy for the athletes once they arrived on site.

Everyone had an opinion about her return, but the only one that mattered was her own. Sure, the sponsors were all here, lining up to see how she'd do. Several offers were already on the table, but with the provision of her finishing in the top three to prove she really was back and capable of skiing professionally again. It was an insult. She worked hard all her life, and then, poof, pins in her leg and knee ended their confidence. *Fickle creatures.*

But today wasn't about the sponsors. This was all about her. And it wasn't about winning. It was about conquering her fear. Fear always had the power of holding someone back, and she didn't want to give in to the emotion. Not that she didn't have it—just that she didn't want to let it control her.

The crowds were becoming standing room only as the events of the day started. Sally had only signed up for the one competition, unwilling to push her body to the point mistakes were made. The downhill race had always been her best and fastest event, and it would be over in less than ninety seconds on this course if she was skiing at her best.

She watched the events as they played out from the TV in the athlete room, cheering on her best friend in the aerial event. Jessica was on point as she flipped a three-sixty, landing the move with precision. Sally clapped excitedly. "Go get 'em, girl," she hollered, not caring who turned to throw her curious glances.

Her dad and Marion approached. "It's time for you to stretch and warm-up. You do know you don't have to do this, right?" her father said.

"Yes, actually, I do need to do this. For me." And for him but telling him as much would only start a discussion she wasn't prepared to have. "You worry like an old man."

"I am an old man...yours," he said, leaning down to kiss her cheek. "I'll be at the bottom cheering you on, sweetheart."

"And I'll be right there with him. Good luck, Sally. You deserve this, and I think after getting to know you the way I have, I know what you're doing. I'll say a prayer for you. Just breathe and relax. And let it come naturally." Marion leaned forward to hug her.

The care and concern touched Sally's heart. It was the closest thing to a motherly hug she had experienced since she was eight. "Wow, you sound more like my coach than my dad." Sally laughed, trying to push away the emotion of the moment. She had a race to focus on and getting all sentimental wouldn't help.

"A mother's intuition covers many areas. Ask my daughter." Marion grinned.

"I'll take your word for it because you might just be on the right track. Thanks for the advice."

"What was that all about?" her father asked as they moved off.

"Nothing. Just girl talk." She watched until they disappeared into the crowd and out of sight. Then, grabbing her gear, she went to check-in for the race.

Sally approached the table near the lift and within minutes had her number, and of course, lots of well wishes. She pulled her assigned number over her ski jacket and was soon heading up the slope on the gondola.

Glancing around, she took in the beauty of the moment. The sun was shining on the hard-packed snow, icing the surface. It was a glorious day. Win or lose, it would be an incredible moment to feel the cold chill of the air on her face. The Birds of Prey was an impeccable course, a favorite of professional skiers. Orange gates twenty-six feet apart lined the route. Sally memorized the curves and swells, searching for the fall line that would take her to the bottom the fastest. It was the only way to do her best. It was what she had been trained to do.

Sweat beaded on her forehead, and she pulled off her beanie, wiping the sweat away with the back of her glove. Her breathing hitched as the line didn't reveal itself. If she couldn't find it, she didn't stand a chance. Closing her eyes, she tried to visualize the path, but it wouldn't come.

The quad lift stopped, and she exited, joining the officials at the top.

It wasn't long before it was her turn.

Sally's heart pounded as she stepped up to the starting line. Images of tripping out the gate the last time flashed in her head, and she tensed. Three deep breaths in and out, she tried to regain control of her emotions. Shoving the images to the dark recesses of her brain, she focused on the slope in front of her and waited for the countdown beeps to begin.

And then she saw it. *The fall line.* Zeroing in on the path, her adrenaline raging in overload.

The countdown beeps started. The green light flashed, and Sally surged forward.

With a 2,100-foot vertical drop, she careened down the slope, edging her skis to cut and turn as she passed through each set of gates. Tucking tight on the straight portions, she focused on her aerodynamics, knowing it was critical to her overall speed.

It was magically freeing. As if she had become one with the mountain and the angels were watching, guiding her along. The warmth of the sun made Sally feel like her mother was there in spirit, smiling and cheering her on. She channeled every last ounce of energy available into her effort to gain speed.

On and on, sheer exhilaration propelled her forward as she carved the slope. Crossing the finish line, Sally held up her ski poles to celebrate. Emotions overflowed by way of tears.

All around her, people cheered, ringing cowbells and clapping, their enthusiasm contagious.

She'd done it. Win or lose, she had competed, and no matter where she placed, Sally considered herself a winner. She had harnessed her fears long enough to do what needed to be done and was rewarded with a special gift from God.

Her mother's presence. It was a memory she would cherish forever.

Punching the air with excitement, Randy let out a whooping yell to celebrate Sally's run. It was an incredible rush as she'd raced down the mountainside, and only now was he able to breathe. He would have liked to let Sally know he was there before she skied. But getting past security wasn't even re-motely possible, something he hadn't con-sidered when he made plans to come to Colorado.

Well-wishers surrounded Sally. Cheers echoed through the area when her scores were posted. She was currently in first place with the best time. It was up to the other skiers to beat her, not the other way around. Randy could almost feel the joy radiating from the glow on her face as she hugged her father and other people, all wanting to share in her success.

The media swarmed around her. It would seem her comeback story was deep in the hearts of people all across the nation. Much the way Randy had been rooting for her, but his reasons were more profound than just a story. It was love for the woman that brought him to Vail.

As Sally walked toward the main building, she glanced his way. Randy waved his arms in the air, hoping she would see him. Instead, a man cut off his view as he joined Sally, one arm going around her waist. The pair stopped to address the media and to pose for photos.

"I didn't know they were back together. He made a mistake leaving in the first place. I reckon he figured it out quick with Sally's comeback," a woman standing not far from him commented.

"They make a handsome couple. Like the ski king and queen of the US," another woman said, seconding the opinion the two were an item.

Randy's heart sank to the pit of his stomach. If she was back with her ex, and by the looks of things, it was true, then there was no reason for him to have come all this way. Yet, part of him still wanted to talk to her, needing more proof.

The man lifted Sally's arm in the air, bringing her hand to his mouth and kissing it. He then leaned down and captured her mouth in a kiss, the media having a field day.

Randy's proof would be all over the papers tomorrow.

Her father was right when he issued the warning. This was Sally's world, and he would be nothing more than a distraction. Randy would never fit in, and he was but a distant memory to her by the looks of things.

It was time to go home. This didn't work out as Randy had hoped, but several good things had come from his military leave. Decision made, he was not reenlisting, preferring to stay in Cedar Grove with Misty. It had occurred to him that it was time for a change in his life with or without Sally. Stability, marriage, and family. That's what he wanted. It was simply a matter of finding the right woman.

In time perhaps, his heart would open to another, but for now, he would focus on finding a home and a job he would love doing.

Chapter Seventeen

♥

SALLY SHOULD HAVE BEEN filled with joy with a gold medal in the downhill event and Christmas just days away. Instead, she sat at her desk, pouring over the endorsement contracts her father had sent over for her to sign.

She picked up the pen...hesitated, then found the line where they needed her signature. Sally hesitated again. The endorsements were what they needed. *If she kept racing.*

If. One single word kept reverberating in her head.

Years of giving everything she had emotionally and physically had taken their toll. It wouldn't be long before she would be pushed out by the next generation of hot shots coming up through the ranks. She thought of the young girls eager for an autograph. *I want to be just like Sally Castle* one of the girls had said. Maybe helping young children develop a love for skiing was a gift she could give back to her fans. So why did she have to get pushed out of the circuit when she could go out a winner?

Sally had proven everyone wrong and her father right. Not only had she returned to skiing, but she'd competed at the top of her game. Her motivation had been pure as she skied with heart, and the results had been stunning. A new women's downhill record for the Birds of Prey course. Something she attributed to her mother's presence.

Her stats were undeniable and something she could be proud of. Helping others follow their dreams would be an incredibly satisfying experience and perhaps just what she needed in her life. *Maybe it was time to retire.* No maybe about it. *It was time.* Sally pushed the contract away and dropped the pen on the desk. She was ready to embrace the opportunity to make changes in her life.

She picked up the phone to face the biggest hurdle of her decision. *Calling her father.*

"Good morning. Did you get the contracts? I promised I'd have them back signed and returned today," her father asked straight away when he answered.

Business as usual. Sally wasn't sure how he'd take the news. Her decision would affect him as much as it would her, but she couldn't keep on the same path she was going. She needed to be honest with him. For the past two years, the joy she once knew had started to fade. "I got them, but we need to talk."

"What's up?"

She took a deep breath and tried to calm her nerves and the butterflies in her stomach. "I'm not sure how to say this, so I'm going to get straight to the point, and I hope you'll understand my decision. I'm quitting the circuit. Retiring. I'm sorry as I know how much this has all meant to you, and that you've given me everything to get here, but I'm not getting any younger, and there's more to life than racing."

Her father's silence was deafening.

Maybe she should have done this in person. She hated to let him down, but if her head wasn't in the game, the slopes were a dangerous place for an athlete. "Say something. Please don't be upset."

"Upset? Hardly. I've always wanted whatever you wanted. So it's just a bit of a shock. Can I ask what's prompting this decision?" he asked, his tone unexpected.

Anger, guilt, and frustration, she would have understood. But calm and concerned...not one bit. "It's been something I've toyed with for years. The last crash definitely played its part. The comeback for me was more to prove to myself I wanted out for all the right reasons. And that I wasn't giving up out of fear."

"And does Randy have anything to do with this decision?" he asked.

Sally was off-kilter with the sudden switch and wasn't sure how to answer. "Yes and no. I like him. A lot. He wanted a shot at a relationship, something I wasn't able to give."

"Interesting." She could almost see her father grinning on the other end of the phone, his satisfied chuckle throwing her another curve. "Sounds to me like you're in love, and I couldn't be happier."

"I'm not sure it matters whether I am or not. Randy was pretty upset with me, and I don't blame him," she added.

"You deserve someone who loves you, not like Bobby, who's too full of himself. He was quick to turn to someone else when he thought you had fallen out of the limelight. I heard he got an earful after the media turned off the cameras."

Sally grinned. "He did at that," Bobby had been a jerk and deserved every last word she laid on him. It was outrageous that he thought they would just pick up where they left off, and she'd go out with him again. For Bobby, it was all about publicity stunts.

"You know, sweetheart, anyone worthy of your love is worth fighting for. And you won't know if you don't try," her father said, his words of wisdom settling somewhere in the vicinity of her heart.

"I know you're right. It's just—"

"No buts. That's fear talking, and the daughter I know who can throw herself down the slope of a mountain at breakneck speeds can handle asking a man if he loves her."

Sally let out a deep breath. "Thanks for the reminder, Daddy. I'll talk to him, but know this, with or without him, I'm retiring."

"What do you want me to tell the endorsers?" he asked.

"Tell them I'll sign, but only on my terms this time around. I've decided to open up a ski school for children, and I think Cedar Grove would be a great place. You can tell them about the school and that it's up to them what brands I choose to promote for the incoming students based on their contract involvement. The money will come in handy to fund the program." It wasn't anything she'd preplanned, but it was the perfect solution. And the sponsor's funds would make the startup of the business a whole lot easier.

"What a great idea. And I know that anything you put your mind to will become a success. I'm behind you one hundred percent."

Sally nodded, feeling much better now than when she picked up the phone. "Like you always have been. I can't thank you enough for all you've done for me over the years."

"It's what I wanted to do, sweetheart. After your mother passed away, I focused on your needs so I wouldn't dwell so much on missing her," he said, his voice rife with emotion.

This was something she hadn't known. The two of them hadn't talked about her mother and the heartache from losing her. Until now. "I know the feeling. It's the same reason I was so committed to skiing. Anything not to think about how much I missed her twenty-four-seven." The conversation was long overdue.

"I'm sure she's proud of you and watching down over us."

"Oh, I know she is. I haven't had a chance to tell you, but she was with me when I flew down that mountain. Her spirit called out to me, and it was a magical moment. I skied for her, and it was the sweetest ride of my life," she said, tears rolling unchecked down her face as she recalled the experience.

"That explains it," her father said.

Not exactly the answer she expected. "Explains what?"

"The glow on your face when you stopped at the bottom. Radiating beauty was the way I thought of it and mentioned as much to Marion."

"What a beautiful thing to say. Thank you, Daddy." More tears fell, and she brushed them away with the back of her hand. "Do you think some of the businesses will go for the school endorsement idea? We need the money."

"*Hmmmph.* I'm sure the sponsors will want a piece of the action as they would be fools if they didn't. But if not, I've got you covered."

Sally shook her head. This would be her business, and her father had done more than enough for her. It was time to stand on her own two feet. Or skis. "I can't ask you to do more. It's time you started focusing on your own life as well."

"First off, there's plenty of money, and investing in you is what I've done all my life, and it gives me great satisfaction. Secondly, I hope you don't mind, but I'm dating Marion, and it's becoming serious," he said, the hesitancy in his voice reminding her of when she called him.

There was no way she would hold him back from love. "I think it's awesome."

"I will always love your mother, but I also think she would want us both to be happy."

"Mom absolutely would. Marion's a lucky lady." Sally meant every word. Her mother was a sweet, loving person filled with the kindest heart. She would never begrudge anyone's happiness.

"I feel like I'm the lucky one. Getting a second chance at love, and at my age? Not anything I saw coming, but I truly believe fate mixed up our breakfast orders to bring us together."

"The Crestfield Inn seems to have brought romance to both of us. Let's just hope my love life goes as well as yours."

"Sounds like you need to book a flight to Vermont."

"And you need to get us some contracts." Sally laughed. "By the way, any interest in partnering with me versus funding me? I could use an Olympian-level coach on my team. Keep this business all in the family."

"Sweetheart, I'm always on your team. Count me in. Got to run, but keep me posted," he said before hanging up.

It was as though a heavy curtain had been lifted, and life was suddenly filled with a joyful light of hope, and with any luck, love.

The shuttle driver pulled up in front of the Crestfield Inn. Sally paid the man and hurried up the walkway. After booking the reservation, she'd caught a flight to Burlington, using the flight time to develop a solid plan of attack. *Operation Humble Pie was ready to begin.*

"Good afternoon, Kyle," she called out, waving at the man as she stepped inside. The warmth and Christmas aroma of pine and cinnamon permeated the air. A fire crackled in the fireplace adding to the intimate setting of holiday cheer.

"Good afternoon. It's great to have you revisit us, Miss Castle."

It was Sally's turn to face up to her decisions and make things right—with everyone. "*Ummm*, yeah, about that. I'm sorry. I hope you understand I had reasons for wanting to remain anonymous."

Kyle shook his head, his smile deepening. "No, no. Don't think another thing about it. What's important is that you're back. Everyone in town was rooting for you when you raced. It was a thrill to watch."

"Thank you." Sally blushed, secretly hoping all her other apologies went this easy. "I need to drop my things off, but do you think I could talk to the chef?"

"I'm sure you can," he said, glancing at his watch and then handing her the metal room key. "He's just finished lunch service and will be closing the restaurant until the dinner preparations begin. I'll let him know you'll be in to see him in a bit. Oh, and you're in room two this time. Up the stairs and to the left. There's a lovely view of the gardens from the room. Or there would be if they weren't covered in snow." Kyle chuckled.

"Thank you so much. I've got a lot to do today, so that would be great if you could arrange the meeting." And it would be even better if the chef agreed to help her. She told her father romance was in the air at the Crestfield Inn, and she could only hope the chef would catch the spirit of her request and help her since it was all in the name of love.

"And hopefully people to see," he asked, grinning and shooting her a wink.

"There is that," she admitted. She headed up the stairs and entered the room. The same feeling of peace washed over her, almost as if it were a homecoming. The inn with all the antiques and looking like it came straight out of the 1700s spoke of history and connections to the past. And she was a part of it now.

Sally freshened up and headed back downstairs.

"Chef is in the kitchen," Kyle announced when she rounded the corner and he spotted her.

"Perfect. Thanks again," Sally said, making her way down the hall to the Garden Delight Bistro. The doors to the kitchen were open, and she went straight in. Finding the chef bent over a masterpiece creation of what looked like dark chocolate mousse with a dark chocolate crust, decorated with whipped cream dabs and raspberry delights and chocolate shavings. *Mouthwatering for sure*. Maybe he would give it to her to take to Randy, and then she wouldn't have to actually cook anything. But then the message wouldn't be the one she wanted to give the man she loved.

Anything worth doing was worth doing right.

"Good afternoon, Miss Castle. How can I help you?" the chef asked, a broad smile lighting his face.

Another friendly face. "You can start by calling me Sally. I'm hoping you can forgive me for not telling you who I was on my last visit?"

His grin deepened. "Of course, Sally. Don't think another thing about it. How can I be of assistance?"

The chef had come from the city, the lure of a small town living a drawcard he hadn't been able to resist. But he had brought his big city recipes to Cedar Grove, and they were local favorites. "I need to bake a pie."

"A pie. Well now, that's an odd request, but easy enough. I don't mind you using my kitchen as long as you clean it up afterward," Chef James said, a teasing grin on his face.

This was the embarrassing part. A grown woman who was as comfortable in a kitchen as a pig would be—eager to escape before messing everything up. "Oh, no. you don't understand. I need you to help me make a pie. I can't cook. And it has to be perfect."

Chef James nodded. "I see. He glanced at his watch. I have some time right now if you're game."

This was going according to plan, and she would make it work. Shoving aside her nerves, she would venture to cook under the tutelage of a master chef. "I am. Thank you so much."

"What kind of pie are you wanting? Perhaps something like this," he asked, pointing to tonight's specialty.

"I was thinking of Humble pie," she said, laying it all out there, unwilling to cower behind her mistakes.

Chef James frowned. "I'm not sure I'm familiar with that one. What's in it?"

Sally shrugged. "Humility. Apology. Friendship. And all rolled into something delicious."

"I see. Sounds like you want out of the doghouse, so to speak?" The sudden twinkling gleam in his eyes as he bit back a smile meant it would be the best Humble pie ever. He totally understood.

"Exactly. I want to deliver it tomorrow morning as a Christmas present." It was only one of the surprises she had in store for Randy, all with the hope he would forgive her and give them a second chance.

"And who's the lucky recipient, or do I even need to ask?" Chef James grinned.

"Randy Granger."

"That's what I suspected. I know just the thing...apple pie has always been a favorite of his when he comes in here, and I just got a bushel of Granny Smith apples from the market yesterday."

It sounded simple enough, but was it too simple? She would trust Chef James on this and prayed he was right. "Wonderful. So where do we begin?"

He pointed toward the sink. "Wash up and put on an apron. I'll get out the ingredients," he said.

"This will be so much fun. Thank you." Maybe she'd even learn a thing or two while she was at it.

"Don't thank me until the pie is out of the oven looking like the best Humble Pie ever." He shot her a wink.

What she wanted was the best pie ever, but more than that, she wanted the recipient to think so also. It was a risk going to his house on Christmas morning, but one she was willing to take.

Hopefully, the holiday spirit would be in full swing.

Chloe twirled around in a circle, excitement bubbling over at Sally's unexpected arrival. Humble pie indeed. It was an excellent plan and bode well for the couple. "I can't believe she's back. It's a miracle," she said, clapping her hands.

"*I do seem to remember telling you it wasn't over,*" Captain Tremont said. "*Not with you pushing them together.*"

"*But this is more like fate.*"

"*A fate you instigated, my dear.*"

"*I like the way you think, my dearest captain.*" Sally was on the right track and the rest was up to Randy. Chloe could only hope he made his decisions with his heart and not his head.

The heart would lead them back to where they belonged—together.

Chapter Eighteen

♥

Christmas morning arrived, Sally's nerves at a breaking point. So much of what she envisioned for her future included Randy. Her ski program would keep her busy if he was deployed again, but the time they spent together would be special. They could make it work, knowing he would be coming home. And with any luck, he could put in for a stateside assignment and try to stay closer.

Of course, all of this depended on his reaction and his answer today. He'd once been about to ask her to be his girlfriend, and Sally was ready to say yes if the offer was still available. But more importantly, she wanted to be friends no matter what. Randy was the kind of person who made one's life richer for having him in it, and there was never a question of his motive or his allegiance.

Something rare in her life up until now, and something she would treasure.

Dressing in a pair of jeans and a warm wool cable-knit sweater, she sat on the bed and pulled out her phone. It was the first Christmas ever without her father, and Sally wanted to talk to him. She pressed the speed dial button and waited. Marion was with him, so it wasn't like he was alone. Which suited Sally just fine. Otherwise, her trip to Cedar Grove might have had to wait a day or two. But then, it was her father who pointed out that when love came knocking, you didn't close the door. Real love was rare indeed.

"Merry Christmas, sweetheart," he said when he answered.

"Merry Christmas, Daddy. I wanted to touch bases with you before I headed over to see Randy."

"Marion and I have already opened our gifts to each other." Her father chuckled. "All four of them."

"Four?" she asked.

"We have everything we need, so for us, it's all about being together with the spirit of Christmas and love filling our hearts with joy."

"That makes me feel better about being away from you this year," Sally said.

"It's all good. How are you holding up?"

"Not as good as you're doing. I'm nervous. What if Randy won't even talk to me?"

"Then he'd be a fool not worthy of my daughter," her father said without a second's hesitation.

"Thank you." He always had a way of making Sally feel better, and this time was no exception. She was ready to face whatever happened today, and she would do it with grace and dignity...and, of course, Humble pie. "On that note, it's time I headed over there. Talk to you later."

"Good luck, sweetheart," her father said before hanging up.

Sally pulled on her fleece-lined winter boots and grabbed her coat. Then, with Randy's Christmas present tucked under one arm and the pie in hand, she headed downstairs.

"Merry Christmas, Sally. Do you need a ride somewhere?" Kyle asked when he spotted her.

"And a Merry Christmas to you as well. Thanks, but I've got the ride covered. Chef James offered me a lift seeing as it was Christmas. If all goes well, I should be back later today. If it goes capooey, I'll walk back and spend Christmas alone." Which wouldn't be much different than all her other Christmas pasts. It just wasn't necessarily what she had hoped for this Christmas.

"You'll be fine. Who could resist such a beautiful lady as yourself?"

"Says the guy not on the receiving end of my deceit. Let's hope you're right," she countered.

Chef James came through the front door, stomping his snow-covered boots on the mat. "Merry Christmas. Are you ready to serve your pie?" he asked, a grin on his face.

"No. Yes. Maybe." Sally laughed. "And Merry Christmas to you. Bye, Kyle," she called out and waved as Chef James held the door open and headed down the steps to his waiting car. The cold morning air made her shiver and all the more grateful for the warm car and ride.

Minutes later, he pulled up in front of the Granger residence. "Are you sure you want me to leave?" Chef James asked.

Sally nodded. "Yes. I'm committed to doing this. All in." She got out of the car and picked up the present and the pie. "Thanks for the ride."

"Well, okay then. Good luck." He drove off, her window of opportunity to change her mind now closed.

Taking a deep breath, she rang the doorbell. Misty barked excitedly on the other side, and it wasn't long before the door was pulled open.

"Sally?" Randy said, his mouth hanging open in stunned disbelief.

"Right in one guess," she said, aiming for humor to offset the tension of the moment. "Merry Christmas." He was in his pajama bottoms and one ugly Christmas sweater...the dancing reindeer complete with a red nose and flashing multi-colored lights. Still, Randy managed to look good with his wavy, just-woke-up hair, only adding to the image. Adorable was the word that came to mind.

"*Ummm*, Merry Christmas to you too. What are you doing here?" he asked, glancing down at the pie.

Sally put on her best smile, one filled with a depth of emotion reserved for Randy. "I have a gift for you. One that needed to be delivered in person." She held her peace offering out to him.

"You bought me a pie?" The lines across his forehead deepened, and he had yet to take her gift.

"No, I *made* you a pie. Well, with help from Chef James," she added, wanting to be totally truthful. Hedging her answers is what got her into this mess in the first place.

"I see. And you came all the way to Cedar Grove to give me a pie," he asked, reaching to take it from her, still sounding unsure of himself.

Or not trusting the face value of the reason for her visit. "No. I also have another gift for you," she said, handing Randy the package.

"You come bearing gifts, but I'm trying to figure out why you're here. Why aren't you in Vail? It's Christmas morning."

Sally wrapped her arms around her midsection to ward off the increasing chill. "Cedar Grove was a better place to spend the holidays. I like it here—a lot. *Especially* the people. Nice sweater, by the way."

Randy looked down at his sweater and frowned. "It's kind of a family thing. So what kind of pie?" he asked, lifting it up to his face and sniffing for any telltale hints.

Now they were getting somewhere. "Humble pie. You know, sort of like your Apology pie, but with an added dollop of humility and a healthy portion of I'm sorry. And I am very sorry. I'd like a chance to explain what happened and why I didn't tell you who I was," she said in a rush, taking full advantage of the opening.

"You rejected my Apology pie." Randy gazed at her with an intensity that rippled all the way down to her cold toes.

"But I also ended up eating it all in one sitting," she pointed out.

Randy smiled. "True. Do you want to come in? The family will be thrilled to see you." He pushed the door open wide and made way for her to enter, assuming her answer would be yes.

"Who's at the door?" his mother called out from behind Randy. Misty bounded into the foyer, jumping excitedly when she spotted Sally. The dog edged closer to the door but looked to Randy for approval to go outside.

"Sally Chas...Castle," he corrected.

"Well, for goodness sake, don't leave her out there in the cold. Invite her in."

"I did, Mother." Randy shook his head, his smile turning into more of a wide grin, complete with the cute crinkles at the corners of his eyes. "Somethings never change."

Sally moved into the foyer, grateful for the reprieve. Randy was giving her a chance to make amends. "And some things do. *I did*," she said, emphasizing the last two words.

Sally dropped to one knee to pet Misty. The dog clearly missed Sally, as much as Sally missed her furball friend.

"What do you mean?" he asked, running a hand through his hair.

Sally stood and moved closer to Randy. "I'm retiring. It's time to start a new chapter in my life. And...and I'm hoping it's a life with you in it," she said, forcing the words out and putting her heart on the line.

"*Wow*. Now that wasn't expected, but I admit, I like the sound of your suggestion. Or at least I think I do. What about Bobby Jackson?"

Misty licked at her hand, vying for attention. "What about Bobby? We aren't a couple, if that's what you're asking. Haven't been since before I met you."

Randy frowned. "The day of your race...I saw—"

"You saw the media in action and Bobby's play for the spotlight. You should have turned the TV off." She was still furious with Bobby for the debacle, but he knew to never darken her doorstep again.

Randy looked uncomfortable as he ran his hands through his hair again. "The thing is, it wasn't the TV."

"Well, then where did you see it? I was furious and gave him a piece of my mind afterward, but it was too late by then. The media had what they wanted—a makeup story. In more ways than one." Sally scowled. It was the part of skiing she hadn't enjoyed.

"I wish I had stuck around long enough to see that part." Randy grinned, suddenly relaxed. His smile was like that of a child on Christmas morning.

But then, it was Christmas morning, so what better time. "You were there? In Vail?" she asked, dumbfounded.

Randy nodded. "I was. I went there to talk to you. About us," he said, closing the distance between them.

She drew in a deep breath. "Is there an us?" she asked, looping her arms around his neck.

"It would seem so." Randy lowered his head and kissed her. A magical Christmas moment for sure. "And oh, by the way, it would seem neither one of us has a job. I retired from the military. So whatever we do, it would seem we both have some free time on our hands."

Sally shook her head. "Not really. I'm already lining up my next venture, but that's wonderful news about you and the military. So what made you decide to get out?"

"I wanted to settle down. Start a new chapter in my life. Just like you are, it would seem. So, where will you be off to this time?" he asked, reaching up to brush her hair back from her face, his thumb grazing her cheek softly.

"Cedar Grove. I'm going to open a ski school for children. Any chance you need a job?" she teased.

"Absolutely," he said, dropping another light kiss on her mouth.

Something she could get used to quickly. "By the way, my dad sends you Christmas greetings. And just so you know, he's also agreed to partner with me in this new business, serving as a coach and instructor."

Randy drew back. "Christmas wishes? Seriously? I didn't think he even liked me."

Sally grinned. "That's because he didn't know you, and he's very protective of his daughter."

"Well, you can tell him you're in good hands. Literally and figuratively," he teased.

Leaning down, Randy kissed her with a tenderness she felt all the way to her toes. *This was love.*

"What are you two doing? Everyone's waiting in the living room," his mother said from the doorway.

They jumped apart.

"Sorry," he mumbled under his breath.

"They're kissing," his mother shouted to all those in the other room, turning their special moment into a family affair.

"Mother...please," Randy groaned.

Sally noted his mother's Christmas sweater and understanding took hold. A family tradition of ugly Christmas sweaters. It was a lovely idea, even if the sweaters were hideous.

Tracy took Sally by the arm and led her into the living room. "Time enough for that later. We've got gifts to open and dinner to get in the oven."

"Sally brought dessert," Randy said as he carried the pie and the gift into the room. "Apple pie," he added. "My favorite."

"So I heard," Sally said, unable to keep from laughing. "Chef James knows you well."

Naomi took the pie from Randy and carried it to the table. After everyone exchanged Christmas greetings and hugs, Sally sat next to Randy on the sofa. He took her hand in his, firmly declaring they were, in fact, together and that his mother hadn't been imagining the kiss.

"When did the sweater tradition get started? And who finds them all?" Sally asked.

"We started this back when Randy and Naomi were young kids, and it stuck. I used to pick them out, but as they got older, everyone got into the spirit of it. Now we all pick out our own, and then after Christmas dinner, we vote on who has the ugliest sweater," his mother explained. "I found this one at a five and dime store in Plattsburgh the day I took the ferry across Lake Champlain with some friends to go bargain shopping."

"I hope you got it for a much-reduced price," Sally teased.

Randy stood. "Wait right here. I almost forgot something," he said, leaving the room and not bothering to wait for an answer.

Moments later, he was back, his warm smile tugging at her heart as he handed her the bag. Sally reached inside and pulled out a sweater. *An ugly sweater*. One with a skinny Santa in his long johns and pom poms of every color on his hat. "*Ummm*, thanks," she said, unsure of what to say. It was nothing she would ever be able to wear, especially not out of the house. She placed it next to her on the sofa.

"Not so fast. You have to put it on." He chuckled. "I bought this so you wouldn't feel left out if you had been here for Christmas, and now you are. I'm glad to see it will officially be entered in this year's contest as it's a doozy." Randy grinned, picking up the sweater and holding it out to her.

Sally nodded, knowing she had little choice. And it was kind of silly fun, something she swore she wanted more in her life.

She slid the sweater over her head, pulling it into place.

"It looks great on you," Naomi teased. Of course, her own sweater looked more than a little ridiculous riding up over her pregnant belly, evening the score.

One by one, the gifts under the tree were opened. It was a family affair; the tradition of watching each other open gifts was a sweet one. It drew out the whole event, allowing time to appreciate what was given and received with love. Sally felt blessed to be a part of this and to be accepted into the group. No one made her feel like a celebrity stopping by for a visit. Instead, this felt real and welcoming—like family. And maybe one day, she would be a permanent part of all this. There was no telling where life would lead her and Randy, but she looked forward to finding out.

Sally rose and went to the tree and re-trieved a small package tucked in at the back. She handed it to Randy.

"What's this?" he asked.

"Just a little something I put in the tree for you before I left town."

Randy opened it, the two potholders a match for the one she bought him earlier. "Perfect. A matched set. You know you can't—"

"Have just one," she finished for him. "That's why I went back and got you more."

"Thank you. The potholders will come in handy since I found a new home and will be moving out soon. Sorry, Mom. I know you like having me here, but a grown man can't live on his mother's couch forever." He hugged his mother.

"Between you, me, and the lamppost, I'm okay with you moving out. Not that I don't enjoy having you around, but if you plan on giving me any grandchildren soon, it's bound to happen." His mother laughed, grabbing her son by the cheek affectionately.

Randy blushed. "Don't go getting ahead of things, Mom."

"I can't believe you already bought a home. When did you do that?" Sally asked.

"At the same time I put in for retirement. It came complete with a white picket fence, so I knew it was the right one." He chuckled.

"I'm with Mom on this. All you need now is a wife," his sister teased, rubbing her belly. "And then a baby. In that order."

"I'll see what I can do." Randy shot Sally a wink. He rose and retrieved the other shopping bag he'd placed under the tree and handed it to her. "Sorry, it's not wrapped. I wasn't expecting you. Although I'm thrilled you're here," he added quickly.

"It's okay, and I'm glad I'm here too." Sally peered inside and discovered the Candy Land game. "What? I can't believe you bought this for me. This is awesome. You do know I'm going to make you play, right?"

"I was hoping," Randy said.

"Are we missing something?" Uncle Willy asked, gazing back and forth between her and Randy. "It's a child's game."

Sally nodded. "It is. I asked Santa for it as a joke when we were at the craft fair. I always wanted this game but never got one as a child. It was always skis or ski-related gifts." But then, it wasn't like she had time for friends either. And friends were not something she could have asked Santa to bring.

"How romantic," his mother said. "A Santa's wish gift. I love it."

"It gets better." Sally stood and retrieved the package she'd brought with her and handed it to Randy.

"Another one?" he asked.

"Yes. This one I bought on the way here, and now, I'm thrilled I did. It's perfect." She was giddy with excitement for him to open his gift and learn her surprise.

"I haven't even opened it yet. Maybe I won't like it," Randy teased, bumping up against her shoulder playfully.

"You will," Sally said with far greater confidence than when she made the decision to buy the gift in the first place. Before she knew she would be sitting here on Christmas Day enjoying the festivities with the man she loved.

Randy pulled back the paper, his laughter ringing throughout the room. "A firetruck. With lights and a siren," he said, turning on the buttons and the sounds filling the air. "This was my Santa's wish for a gift."

"Talk about a match made in heaven." His mother laughed. "We're so glad you're here, my dear. This is the happiest we've seen Randy since you left. Happiest in forever, for that matter."

"Thank you, what a sweet thing to say. I don't plan on leaving again either as I'm moving to Cedar Grove," Sally announced to everyone in the room.

"Best news ever." The family took turns to hug and welcome her to town.

It took a leap of faith to get here, but she had clearly found where she belonged. With God and her mother guiding her along the way, she couldn't fail.

After dinner and dessert, Sally was more than ready for a breathing space, and she needed some time to talk to Randy. *Alone.* They made their excuses and headed for the Crestfield Inn.

Randy held the door open as they entered the lobby hand in hand.

"Well, well. It looks like Humble pie was a huge hit," Kyle said, grinning.

"Best pie ever," Randy agreed. "Merry Christmas."

"Merry Christmas to you also. And what wonderful news. But then I was sure it was a grand plan and not one you would let pass up. Miss Castle is a special woman."

"I couldn't agree more," Randy said, kissing her cheek.

"Kyle, you've been here all day. Why aren't you spending time with someone special?" Sally asked, concerned for her new friend.

Kyle shrugged. "There's no one special in my life right now. I love the inn and sharing joy and happiness with the guests staying here." The hint of wistfulness in Kyle's tone said there was more to his answer than he let on.

"I see." Kyle was too friendly of a guy not to find his own special someone, but if there was one thing Sally had learned, love came to those who waited.

"So when is the wedding? Surely you'll have it right here at the inn," Kyle asked, changing the subject.

Sally shook her head and smiled. "That's getting ahead of us. We've only just agreed to give this a go. But it's looking good for pies and promises," she said, laughing. "You should advertise the inn as a place where romance abounds. Even my father fell in love with the woman he met here. Could be great for business."

"What a splendid idea. I'll mention it to Mr. Montpelier. There have been a lot of chance meetings and new-found loves lately."

Chloe held up her arms, and Captain Tremont stepped forward to pull her close. "We did it," she exclaimed as he spun her around.

"I never doubted you'd be successful for a moment. You have a way of sensing who belongs together and who doesn't." Captain Tremont chuckled, stepping back to bow low.

"I was a bit worried when Sally left. Sometimes the anticipation and not knowing what happened is enough to drive me crazy. But when she came back to the inn, I held out great hope."

"Well, in this case, it was worth the wait. Not only did you find out you were right about Sally and Randy, but it sounds like your bit of two-stepping with the breakfast tickets put Addison Castle and Marion together. That's a two-for-one deal." He grinned.

"A bonus romance. Works for me. The world needs more love. Oh, and speaking of romance...Sally said something, and it got me thinking," Chloe said, one finger tapping her lip.

"What's that, my dear?"

"Kyle. After things ended with that girl Rachel, he's here working all the time...even today. It's Christmas. I want to make sure that changes by next year. He's a nice man who deserves true love."

"Watch out Kyle. You're officially on Miss Chloe's matchmaking radar." Captain Tremont's deep chuckle echoed through the room.

"Phooey. You say it like it's a bad thing," she popped him lightly against his shoulder to rebuke his statement.

"Never, my love. With the right woman, love is always a good thing."

"See that you remember that Captain Tremont," she said, taking his arm.

They lingered a moment longer before heading up the stairs to the attic. Tonight they would dance twice as long to celebrate the double win in the romance column.

Epilogue

One year later...

Randy was excited for Sally's arrival, eager to present the first of his gifts. A Love Pie. This was the first Christmas in his new home. It would be an extra memorable holiday if everything went right, the second of many they would share together for years and years to come. Perhaps even with their children.

Sally stayed late last night as it was Christmas Eve, which meant Randy had been up quite a bit longer baking. It was only fitting he propose with a pie, seeing as every significant event they shared seemed to involve pie. A tradition he was a huge fan of, considering his penchant for dessert.

Placing the pie behind the tree on a table, he made sure everything was perfectly in place. The ring box was on the top, tied off with a bow. The words "Will you marry me?" were etched in red icing to match the cherry filling.

It hadn't taken him long after they got together for him to know he loved her and that she was the one he wanted the whole family plan with, right down to the white picket fence. But he'd waited to make it known because things had been a bit hectic between Sally moving into town, renting a house near the resort, and getting her business off the ground. And this was a moment he wanted to savor.

"Merry Christmas," Sally called out loudly from the front foyer. "I'm here."

As always, her arrival brought him great joy. Lost deep in thought, he hadn't heard the front door open and close, and he quickly stepped away from the tree. His heart raced, knowing the moment was upon him.

"Merry Christmas, darling," he said, stepping forward to take some of the bags from her, putting them on the living room sofa while she removed her jacket. Misty had joined them and barked excitedly, her tail wagging and thumping against the wall as she waited for her own personal greeting from Sally.

"When are the others due to arrive?" she asked. "I think my dad and Marion won't be here until around ten."

"I think they said nine-ish. Which works for me because then I have you all to myself for an hour before the others get here and take over the house." Randy laughed. Sally moved under the mistletoe he'd hung last night. "Stop right there," he said quickly, holding up his hand.

"Why? What's wrong?" Sally glanced around.

Randy pointed to the top of the doorway. "Tradition says I must kiss the girl." He grinned and stepped closer.

"Nice move. As long as I'm the only girl you go around kissing under the mistletoe," she teased.

"The one and only." He took Sally in his arms, lowering his mouth to hers. This was no ordinary Christmas kiss...this was the kiss of a man in love and about to propose.

"Wow. That's some greeting. Maybe we should leave the mistletoe up year-round."

Sally's easy laughter and warm-hearted spirit were always a joy to him. "I'm hoping we won't need it." Randy took her by the hand and led her to the Christmas tree. He reached behind it and brought around the pie, using his body to shield what he was doing from her view.

"What's going—oh..." she said, as he dropped to one knee and held up the pie.

"Now that your ski school is open and quite successful, I figure it's time to focus more on us. I love our traditions, and this one's called a Love pie. Cherry since it's your favorite. I love the life we're building together. But most of all, I love you. Will you marry me, Sally Castle, and spend the rest of your life with me?"

Tears rolled down Sally's face, joy etched in her expression. In his heart, he already knew the answer, but he held his breath, waiting for her response.

She reached for the box and opened it, the diamond twinkling from the lights on the tree as she pulled it from the velvet-lined tray and handed the ring to him. "Yes, I'll marry you. Forever and ever because I love you too. Something you know, but I want to keep on telling you every day."

Randy slid the ring on her finger and then rose, kissing her again, this time as his fiancée. When he lifted his head, he gazed down at her. "See what I mean? Mistletoe not required," he teased.

She flung her arms around his neck. "Just as long as you make it a tradition to kiss me every chance you get."

"I'll make sure of it. I've thought about this a lot, and I'm hoping you'll agree with my one special request. I don't want a long engagement because I'm ready to start my life with you. Now and forever."

Sally nodded. "I'm totally on board with that, Mr. Granger."

"We can get married at the Crestfield Inn just like Kyle mentioned last Christmas, seeing as that's where we met," Randy suggested, pressing the issue. A spring wedding would be perfect there, especially with the flowers starting to bloom and matching his bride's radiant beauty.

"Actually, we met at the top of a blue run on the mountain, but I don't relish getting married there. However, I agree we should consider the Crestfield Inn as our magical place because that's where you first showed up at my door with an Apology pie. That took real courage, and it was when I first started to care about you, even if I didn't want to at the time."

"I think it was more a case of you liking my culinary skills. I think I remember you saying you ate the whole thing." Randy teased.

Sally grinned. "Hey, I was upset at a lot of things. Lots of people overeat when they are upset. Besides, it was delicious."

"It's settled then. A wedding at the Inn. And you could even ask Jennifer and Laura to be your flower girls. They are some of your biggest fans and best students."

"What a great idea. I do, however, have one special request to make. My father is planning to ask Marion to marry him today, and he mentioned the Crestfield Inn as a venue. It sounds like another family tradition could be starting, but...I don't want this to be a double wedding. I want it to be our own special day."

"I like the sound of that. And perhaps, a Love pie will be in order for every anniversary," Randy suggested, always happy when more pie opportunities arose. At least, the happy pies.

"No perhaps about it, Mr. Granger." Sally grinned.

Randy took her in his arms, and they danced to the Nutcracker Suite music playing in the background. Misty ran in circles around them, barking, trying to get their attention...or maybe she understood and was giving a canine blessing to the engagement.

This year, Randy's Christmas wish to Santa at the craft fair had been a special request. And it would seem the jolly old man had delivered.

A Christmas to remember and a fiancée who loved him.

What's Next?

If you enjoyed the heartwarming fun at the Crestfield Inn...be sure to check out the
<u>Holidays in Hallbrook collection</u>
for year-round holiday happiness!

For awesome Happily-Ever-After Sweet Romances, be sure to check out **ALSO BY ELSIE DAVIS**. And if you like Christian Inspirational Western Romance...be sure to check out the new **CROSSROADS CREEK COWBOYS**! Cowboys down on their luck, love, and laughter, who get a second chance at happiness.

The greatest compliment you could give an author is to leave a review in order to help other readers discover the same great stories you enjoyed. Amazon/Bookbub/Goodreads are all great places. Many thanks!!!

Want to keep in touch with new releases and what's happening in the world of Elsie Davis? *Sign up for the monthly newsletter here... Elsie Davis HEA (Happily-Ever-After)* And while you're there, check out the new Elsie Davis Bookstore for direct sales at a discounted price.

Another great way to keep in touch - *Follow Elsie Davis on FaceBook*

Also By Elsie Davis

Sweet, Clean and Wholesome Stories...with a Happily-Ever-After Guarantee!

Holidays in Hallbrook
(Sweet Romance Series for Holidays Throughout the Year)
Welcome to Hallbrook, New Hampshire. A small-town filled with the unexpected, lots of love, and of course, a beloved dog to ramp up the excitement.
Love & Order (Labor Day)
Love & Family (Thanksgiving)
Love & Peace (Christmas)
Love & Chocolate (Valentine's Day)
Love & Hope (Mother's Day)
Love & Liberty (Independence Day)
Love & Honor (Veteran's Day)
Love & Joy (Easter)

Love & Adventure (Father's Day)

Great Smoky Mountain Getaways
(Christian Inspirational – Women's Fiction Romances)
Juliet's Journey to Love
Poppy's Path to Love
Rachel's Road to Love

Crossroads Creek Cowboys
(Christian Inspirational Romances)
The Heart of a Cowboy
The Help of a Cowboy
The Return of a Cowboy
Coming Soon – The Care of a Cowboy

Crestfield Inn Romances
**If you like special kinds of soulmates,
a splash of the supernatural, and wholesome relationships, you'll adore this sweet
bit of fun filled with romance and mystery.**
Turning Back Time
Turning Up Roses

Turning Down Pie

Celebrity Corgi Romance
(Standalone Sweet Romance)
If you like light mystery mixed in with your happily-ever-after, you'll enjoy this second-chance romance and the race to save an adorable Corgi.
Digging the Driver

Gold Coast Retrievers
(Sweet Romance)
Special Golden Retrievers help their humans solve mysteries, save lives, and even find love...
Defending Dakota

Trinity River
(Sweet Western Romance)
Ranchers and farmers depend on the Trinity River for water, but when a secret conglomerate starts buying up property by fair means or foul, it's time for the landowners

*of Tumble County to fight back—Texas style.
But what they don't count on, is finding love
in the process.*
Back in the Rancher's Arms
Small Town, Big Secrets

Coming Soon! (2023-2024)

Sundancer's Legacy – 9 Book series

Sundancer's Star
Sundancer's Joy
Sundancer's Heart
Sundancer's Majesty
Sundancer's Miracle
Sundancer's Glory
Sundancer's Kiss
Sundancer's Moon
Sundancer's Splendor

Elsie Davis is a *USA Today and International Bestselling Author* of over 25 sweet, clean, and wholesome romances, and a member of the ACFW. She discovered the world of Happily-Ever-After romance at the age of twelve when she began avidly reading Barbara Cartland, the Queen of Romance, and has been hooked ever since. After building her dream log home on top of a small mountain, she turned her attention to do what she loves most, writing. Elsie writes sweet Contemporary Romance and Contemporary Christian Romance from her heart...hoping to share a little love in a big world.

When she's not writing, she can be found birding, kayaking, camping, fishing, playing disc golf, and taking nature walks—hoping to spot wildlife. Basically, she loves all things outdoors, EXCEPT cold weather. She and her husband are avid Caribbean cruisers, but Elsie's favorite vacation was their cruise to Alaska. (In spite of the cold!) Indoors, she enjoys a toasty fire, and of course, a great romance with a guaranteed Happily-Ever-After.

https://www.elsiedavishea.com